P.C. HAWKE mysteries

THE GOURMET ZOMBIE

- - - - - - - - -

P.C. HAWKE
mysteries

THE GOURMET ZOMBIE

- - - - - - - -

PAUL ZINDEL

VOLO
Hyperion
New York

Copyright © 2002 by Paul Zindel

Volo and the Volo colophon are trademarks of Disney Enterprises, Inc.
All rights reserved. No part of this book may be reproduced or transmitted in any form or by any means, electronic or mechanical, including photocopying, recording, or by any information storage and retrieval system, without written permission from the publisher. For information address Volo Books, 114 Fifth Avenue, New York, New York 10011-5690.

Printed in the United States of America
First Edition
1 3 5 7 9 10 8 6 4 2

The text for this book is set in Janson Text 11.5/15.
Photo of thunderstorm: Don Farrall

Library of Congress Catalog Card Number on file.
ISBN 0-7868-1590-6
Visit www.volobooks.com

Contents

Case #7 began something like this:

At exactly 1:13 on the afternoon of Saturday, March 27, a bowl of Caesar salad was placed in the hands of an up-and-coming chef named Billy Rose, star of the hit cooking show, *The Undressed Chef*. The tightly packed crowd of onlookers in front of the Plaza Hotel in New York City cheered enthusiastically as the young chef took his first bite. A tourist from Germany, who was filming the scene from across the street, chortled in Bavarian amusement when Rose suddenly clutched his throat and started jerking back and forth like a marionette in the hands of a crazed puppeteer.

Seconds later, the crowd's laughter turned to cries of horror when it realized that Rose was not *pretending* to be poisoned. From the flecks of foam forming at the corners of his mouth and the ghastly blue pallor of his face, it had become obvious that Rose was in his death throes. He was as white as undressed tofu.

The scene exploded into chaos as celebrity chefs, police officers, and paramedics milled about onstage while the crowd fought the conflicting impulses to 1) flee in terror, and 2) rush forward to rubberneck the gruesome sight.

It was quite a kickoff to the twelfth annual New York Is Food Country festival. Sure, American cooking is famous for being 4F—fast, frozen, and fat free. But, as my best bud and detective partner, Mackenzie Riggs, and I soon discovered, they'd left out a few more Fs—like the ones for frightening, frenzied, felonious, and fatal. And when we got involved in the case, we never expected that a masked zombie killer was going to be dishing out additional helpings of death. Or that Mac and I were slated to be on the menu!

Recording the truth and nothing but the truth, I am,

C. C. Hawke

(a.k.a. Peter Christopher Hawke)

The Silence of the Clams

"Hurry up, P.C.! We're going to be late for the festival." Mackenzie took me by the arm and yanked me down Fifth Avenue.

"Hold on a sec." I had come to a complete standstill in the middle of the block as I watched a Boston terrier dressed in green surgical scrubs trot by wearing teeny-tiny booties on all four paws. I couldn't move until I got a look at its owner. I just had to know what kind of weirdo would do that to a dog. One day, my curiosity is going to be my downfall. But until then, I intended to give it full rein.

Mackenzie groaned, but parked on the corner anyway, tapping one of her leopard-print Doc Marten–shod feet at supersonic speed—her way of letting me know that I only had a split second before she ditched me.

"It's so fab and brill that your aunt and uncle are renting Chelsea Piers for our birthday, P.C.," she said. "We're going to have the greatest party in the history of Westside High."

"Ummh," I grunted, still on the lookout for the dog's owner.

Westside is the private school Mac and I go to. Half the kids there are SRF—Spawn of the Rich and Famous. So having the best birthday party ever would be a major coup, considering the budgets that some of our classmates have to work with. For instance, Anna Green, whose mom is a bigshot TV producer, had her sweet-sixteen party at the Rainbow Room. And Joey Darzano's parents rented an entire Staten Island Ferry and served caviar linguine and all the mesquite shrimp you could eat.

For some reason, Mac was obsessed with topping Anna and Joey and all the rest of them. So she'd asked my aunt Doris, who happened to be best friends with Mrs. Lester, the booking agent of star chef Julius LaCroix, if she could call in a favor and get the great man himself to cater our party. Aunt Doris had said she'd work on it. In the meantime, she'd scored us two backstage passes for the opening ceremonies of the New York Is Food Country festival, where Julius LaCroix would be performing live. And we could check out the other top chefs, too, just in case he said no.

I took one last look around. Aha! Pay dirt. A thin, gray-haired man dressed in a suit, surgical mask, and white gloves scooped up the terrier and marched down the street, ignoring all the pointing tourists, and being ignored—for the most part—by his fellow New Yorkers. Curiosity satisfied, I grabbed Mac by the hand and broke into a trot. "Let's go!"

"Why the big hurry all of a sudden?" she said.

"We want to get there in time to meet Julius LaCroix, don't we?" I said. "If we can talk him into doing our party, there's no way Nicole Venuto won't come."

"Nicole Venuto?" Mackenzie spat out the name as if it were poison. "We're not inviting that ditzy, two-faced, Britney Spears look-alike, are we?" She tossed her long blond hair over her shoulder. "Seems to me much more important that Sutton Van Dusen shows up."

"Sutton No Cluesen?" I sputtered, coming to a halt. "Sutton Vac Cumen? That airhead? He's got the mental capacity of a stapler. A *broken* stapler! A broken stapler with no staples in it! If you want *him* to come, you'll have to ask him in person, because he won't be able to read the invitation."

Mac reached up and whomped me on the head. "Watch what you say, P.C. It just so happens that he asked me out last week. And I just might accept." With that, she took off across the intersection just as the lights changed, leaving me stranded on the curb.

I caught up with her on the southeast corner of Central Park. "Hey, Mac, it's okay if you want to invite Sutton Van Doofus. Really." After all, I thought, he might get lost and fall off the pier.

Mackenzie smiled. I knew all was forgiven. Then she said, "Come on, let's take the shortcut through the Plaza."

Grand Army Plaza, with its huge gold statue of General Sherman on his rearing horse, was packed with people milling around, waiting for the festivities to start. Getting to the stage by the direct route was a losing proposition, but Mac and I hadn't grown up in the City for nothing. We circled around to the Clam Bar entrance at the back of the Plaza Hotel, cut through the hallways past the Palm Court, and came out on Fifty-ninth Street, directly behind the stage. An oversized bald-headed guy checked our passes and waved us through to a special roped-off area on the north side of the stage, where a bunch of folding chairs had been set up.

Mackenzie and I stumbled to our seats, which were only about twenty feet from where the chefs would be performing. On the way, we tripped over journalists, photographers, and other pass holders who were probably friends of the chefs. Or nephews of friends of the booking agents of the chefs, as the case may be.

"Whew! Made it," I said, finally plopping into my seat and looking around.

It was a circus. Loudspeakers were blaring cheesy food-themed songs like "Animal Crackers," "Tangerine," and "American Pie." The crowd was buzzing like mutant bees in an equally cheesy fifties sci-fi movie. The celebrity chefs would be arriving at any minute.

Onstage, a familiar-looking woman in a black pantsuit was click-clacking around in stiletto heels, snapping at techies and propmen and assistant chefs. Her glossy blond hair was pulled back in a neat bun, and not a hair was out of place.

Mackenzie nudged me. "Look, P.C. There's Deborah Hudson, the mayor's ex. I read that she'd be in charge of the festival this year."

"She looks like one of those mannequins in the windows at North-Astor's," I observed. And we should know. Mac and I had discovered a body in the department store's window once. For three days, thousands of people walked by and didn't notice the body. Mackenzie and I knew it was a corpse the minute we clapped eyes on it. It had been our very first case.

"Yeah," Mackenzie agreed. "She's pretty slick."

From our seats so close to the action, we could see the assistant chefs cooking up a storm. Delicious smells started wafting over us, and my mouth started watering. "Mmmm . . . smells delish. Pretty soon, we'll find out whose cuisine reigns supreme," I said.

"It's not *Iron Chef*, P.C.," Mackenzie said. "They're not going to be competing—just doing a little demonstration."

At that moment, a shiny yellow vintage Checker cab—the kind you see in old movies like *Breakfast at Tiffany's*—pulled up to the curb. It was probably the last one left in New York. A tall woman in a floor-length black satin evening gown got out, followed by an oversized goon in a black, double-breasted suit, and waved a white-gloved hand to the crowd. "Darlings!" she croaked. The audience roared in response.

Her raspy voice made me wince and wonder if she'd inhaled too much smoke in the kitchen over the years. "Who's that?" I asked Mackenzie. "And how the heck does she cook in that getup?"

Mac pulled a dog-eared copy of *Gotham Gourmet* out of her backpack and slapped it down on my knee. "Honestly, P.C., do I have to do *all* the research? It's your party, too."

I yanked open the magazine and speed-read the article about the top five chefs in the city. There was only one woman in the top five. So I took a wild guess. "Vladimira Koncharovna, head chef of I, Caviar, right?"

"Bingo!"

We watched as Vladimira mounted the stage. The goon took up position at the side of the stage near us, crossed his arms, and glared at us all from underneath his bushy unibrow. Vladimira launched an air-kiss two feet away from Deborah Hudson's glossy face.

"Deborah! Darling! Still burning your scandals at both ends, dear?" we heard her say.

Deborah air-kissed back. "Vladimira, so nice to see you. You're looking fabulous . . . for a person of your age!"

Vladimira let out a rasping belly laugh. "Deborah, Deborah, Deborah. When I was thirty, I wondered what people would think of me. Now I wonder what *I* think of *them*." And she looked Deborah up and down as if to say, *not much*.

It was cool having front-row seats. We could hear everything that was going on onstage. It was like sitting on the floor of Madison Square Garden during Knicks games.

"Look at the fake smiles on their faces," I said.

"Those aren't smiles," Mac said. "They're baring their teeth at each other."

Vladimira took her place on a chair at the back of the stage and Deborah minced away to welcome the new arrival, who was just pulling up in a black stretch limousine. A tough-looking, red-haired guy leaped out of the limo and bounced up the steps to the stage. He played to the crowd, bobbing and weaving, throwing quick jabs and showing some fancy footwork like a welterweight practicing his shadowboxing. The audience whistled and made woofing noises. In response, he made the palms-to-the-sky pushing motion to "raise the roof." The crowd screamed deliriously, and a gaggle of girls who looked about our age went swarming up to get his autograph.

I glanced down at *Gotham Gourmet*. "Danny Moran, 'The Turf Club Stud,' I presume?"

"Yup," Mac said. "And forget it, P.C. No way is he catering our party. Big hunks of meat isn't my idea of an impressive spread."

"Not mine, either. Give me a little credit, Mac."

Deborah Hudson greeted Danny Moran with a kiss. But unlike the one she'd airmailed to Vladimira, we were interested to see that this one landed smack on Danny's lips.

"Hey, babe," Danny said. "Looking good."

"Thank you for coming, Danny," she said. Then she leaned in and whispered something in his ear. Whatever she said, it must have been interesting, judging by Danny's reaction.

"I get the feeling Deborah and Danny are more than just friends," I observed.

"Well, there was that item in 'Page Six' in last week's *Post*," Mac said.

Deborah took hold of Danny's arm and ushered him to the back of the stage. "Why don't you sit next to Vladimira, Danny."

"Danny," said Vladimira in her raspy voice. "What a pleasant surprise."

"Wouldn't of missed it for the world, Vlad old girl."

"I read the article on you in the *Times* last month, Danny," Vladimira said. "You know, the one where you said you were the architect of your own success."

"Yeah, that was a nice little piece," Danny said. "What did you think of it, Vladi?"

"I said to myself, how fortunate for Danny that the building inspectors weren't around during the construction." Vladimira tittered at her own witticism.

Danny shrugged off her attempts to get under his skin. "You love me, don't you, Vlad baby?" he said loudly, slapping her so hard on the back that she gave a little cough. Off to the side, her goon/bodyguard made an abrupt movement as if he were going to charge the stage and rip Danny's face off.

But apparently, Vladi baby could take care of herself. "Try that again, Danny boy, and you'll draw back a stump." Her voice was as cold as a screeching wind on an Arctic tundra.

Danny laughed, but he looked a little pasty, like uncooked dough.

"Man, that Vladimira's scary," I said to Mackenzie.

"They don't call her the Russian Wolfhound for nothing," Mac said.

A few minutes later, the next chef arrived in a pink Cadillac convertible. He was draped in an ankle-length white ermine coat and wore oversized purple-framed glasses that would not have looked out of place at an Elton John concert circa 1974. As he waved to the audience, we were nearly blinded by the sunlight reflecting off his ring-laden fingers.

"I thought you said this wasn't *Iron Chef*, Mac. What's Chairman Kaga doing here?" I said, referring to the flamboyant, Liberace-like host of the popular show.

"That's Paul Zachary, owner of The Season of the Dove, on Park Avenue. My parents went there for their anniversary last year."

Paul Zachary walked slowly up onto the stage, waving and bowing to the crowd, taking his time. After a brief chat with Deborah, he made his way over to where the other chefs were seated, and was greeted by Vladimira Koncharovna and Danny Moran in snarky fashion.

"Paul, darling!" said Vladimira. "I haven't seen you since . . . why, yesterday, when I noticed your face on a box of cornflakes at the A&P. But then I realized that it wasn't Chef Paul flogging flakes, it was some ghastly footballer."

"Natural mistake for someone of your advanced years to make," Zachary replied. They air-kissed with the same lack of affection that Vladimira and Danny Moran had shown each other.

Danny stepped forward and grabbed Zachary's hand. I could hear the rings grinding together from where I sat. "Yo, what's cooking, buddy?" Danny said.

Zachary grimaced and sniffed. "Something a tad more refined than a slab of beef."

Danny laughed off the jibe and gave Zachary a hearty whack on the back. Zachary stumbled forward from the force of the blow, caught himself, and laser-beamed Danny with his eyes. After a full second blast, he sat down and started smoothing down the fur of his coat. All three chefs then clammed up, ignoring each other.

"I had no idea cooking was a contact sport," I said.

"Or a snapping contest," said Mackenzie. "Oh, and we're *not* letting Paul Zachary near our party. Think how many poor animals had to die to make that coat of his."

I patted her on the shoulder. She was practically

vibrating, she was so mad. "Okay, Mac. We won't let Chairman Kaga cater our party."

I got the feeling Mac was on the verge of rushing up to the stage, whipping out her lipstick, and going to town on the coat. Luckily, a humongous olive-green camouflage Hummer pulled up just then. The door opened, and we could see the impressive figure of Julius LaCroix. With him was a younger man who helped the chef step out of the gigantic vehicle, then handed him a silver-tipped cane.

"Check it out," I said.

If there was one chef in the whole world that even a nonfood fanatic like me would recognize instantly, it would be Julius LaCroix. He'd had a cooking show on P.B.S. since I was a little kid. *The Gourmet Zone* had been a top-ten prime-time hit for years. He waved and smiled at the crowd, who gave him a long and respectful ovation.

As he limped past us, Mac leaped up and held out her hand. "Excuse me, Mr. LaCroix? I wanted to thank you for the guest passes Mrs. Lester gave us. I'm Mackenzie Riggs, and this is my friend, P.C. Hawke."

The chef paused, leaning heavily on the silver-tipped cane, and shook Mac's outstretched hand. "You're quite welcome, my dear. So glad you could make it." The guy who had helped him down from the Hummer smiled at us, then continued to walk the chef toward the stage.

Mackenzie say down and clutched my arm. "Oh my God, P.C. We could actually have the number-one chef in New York cater our party! Everyone at school will just die of envy."

"Sure, Mac, sure," I said, humoring her. I'd never seen her get so worked up before. She usually didn't care what people thought—as was obvious from the way she dressed. I wondered if it was because she wanted to impress Sutton Van Doofus, or if it was because she wanted to put one over on Nicole Venuto.

By this time LaCroix had managed to clump up the stairs, with help from his assistant. Deborah Hudson came skittering over and said, "Monsieur LaCroix, I'm so pleased you could come." She grabbed his hand and pumped it up and down.

"My pleasure, Miss Hudson," said LaCroix in his deep, familiar voice. "You know my assistant, Robbie McGrath?"

"Of course," said Deborah, giving him a fake, animatronic smile. "And I'm *very* familiar with his book, of course."

Robbie pointedly ignored Deborah, turning his back on her as he helped Julius across the stage.

Mackenzie raised her eyebrows at me. I waggled mine back.

Julius greeted the other chefs as Robbie left him and came down to sit a few seats away from Mac and me. "Vladimira," he said. "I hope you had a pleasant vacation in Moscow. Imagine, thirty full days in subzero temperatures. Only *you* could thrive there!"

Vladimira bared her teeth, not even pretending she didn't loathe the man. "And I'm so glad your operation went well. I heard they had to give you four pig valves. Tell me, what does it feel like to have the heart of a swine?"

"Better than having the soul of a cockroach, I'm sure," Julius replied. Turning to Danny, he said, "Ah, Mr. Moran. Too bad you weren't able to get the lease on that new restaurant out on Long Island. The Hamptons could use more of your kind of food. At the present there's only McDonald's and Burger King to choose from."

"Julius, buddy, you're a real card," Danny said, laughing his insincere laugh.

As Julius reached Paul Zachary, we wondered what his opening shot would be. But he limped by him, and pointedly failed to acknowledge his existence. The old chef finally reached his seat at the far end of the stage. As soon as he did, one of the assistant chefs who'd been cooking away in the background came rushing over and plopped himself down next to him.

"Mac, who's that guy talking to Julius? It looks like Julius is about ready to chew his own foot off to get away."

"Hmmm . . . he looks sort of like the chef on that new show, *The Undressed Chef*. Billy somebody."

"He cooks naked?"

"No, dummy. The *food's* undressed—meaning no rich sauces—not the chef."

Before I could get back at her for calling me a dummy, Deborah Hudson stepped up to a microphone, tapped it, and waited for the feedback to die out.

"Welcome to the twelfth annual New York Is Food Country festival!"

Stick a Fork in Him, He's Done

More cheering, whistling, screaming. On either side of the stage, two big bunches of red and white balloons shot into the clear blue sky.

"My name is Deborah Hudson, and, as head of the New York Food Council and coordinator of the festival, I would like to introduce our chefs, in order, as voted by readers of *Gotham Gourmet*."

Deborah Hudson introduced, in turn, number four: Danny Moran; number three: Vladimira Koncharovna; number two: Paul Zachary; and finally, Julius LaCroix.

I turned to Mac. "What is this, Miss America?"

"Yeah, maybe it *is* a competition. No wonder they're at each other's throats."

At the mic, Deborah Hudson continued, "To kick off this year's festivities, I've asked each of our chefs to help prepare a delectable salad using the ingredients on the table in front of us. In honor of the number-one chef in New York, we're calling it a *Julius* Caesar Salad."

The audience groaned good-naturedly at the corniness of the joke. Julius mugged for the crowd, pretending to be hurt by their reaction. The groans changed to cheers, and Julius waved and smiled.

Turning to him, Deborah, said, "Chef LaCroix, would you like to describe the ingredients?"

Julius, hobbling with his cane, took the microphone from Deborah. "Certainly, my dear," he boomed. "No traditional Caesar of mere romaine for me. Here we have a bowl of beautiful baby greens—arugula, radicchio, Bibb lettuce. We have walnuts, sliced Bartlett pears, blue cheese, anchovies, beets. Sunflower seeds, hard-boiled eggs, all kinds of delicious-looking fixings. And last, but not least, my famous secret Caesar salad dressing."

He handed the mic back to Deborah, then returned to the end of the table. "Thank you, Chef," said Deborah. "Now, I'd like Danny, on the end, to take a salad plate, put an ingredient on it, and pass it on to Ms. Koncharovna, who'll add another ingredient and pass it on to Mr. Zachary. And Mr. Zachary will pass it to Chef LaCroix. Chef, when you're finished, you hand the plate to me—and *I* get to eat it!"

The crowd laughed uproariously.

"I'm joking!" Deborah cried, spotlights reflecting off her million-dollar blond hair. "What do you say, people? Do our wonderful chefs deserve the first salads?"

Everyone cheered wildly.

"Wonderful! Chef LaCroix will have the honor of eating first, and the other chefs will follow. Then, if you're good," she said to the audience, "I'll pass salads to some lucky folks out there. Everyone ready?"

The chefs all nodded, and the crowd cheered enthusiastically.

"Let's make some salads!"

Very theatrically, Danny Moran picked up the first salad plate and dumped some greens onto it. He handed the plate to Vladimira, who sprinkled sunflower seeds on top. Paul Zachary made a big show of trying to decide what to add, finally settling on a spoonful of croutons.

When the salad plate finally came to Julius, he added a dollop of salad dressing, stumbling slightly as he held the plate in one hand and his cane in the other. Luckily, the dressed undressed chef, Billy, who was still clinging to Julius's side like a leech, managed to steady him.

At the microphone, Deborah Hudson said, "It looks like our chefs are starving! Chef, why don't you help yourself to a delicious bite."

Julius lurched to the table and added one more finishing touch: a spoonful of walnuts. Then he plunged a fork into the salad, drew out a huge mass of greens and dressing, and opened his mouth. He paused, waving his fork and teasing the salivating crowd. Everyone pretended to beg for a taste.

Billy shouted, "Me! Me! I'm starving!"

"Of course you are," said Julius. "And I insist you go before me. Beauty before age, you know." He handed the fork and salad plate to Deborah Hudson, who was standing next to Billy. "Please pass this along to my new young friend, Billy Rose, star chef-to-be."

Smiling for the crowd, Deborah handed the fork and plate to Billy, who gratefully made a big show of sliding the mass of greens into his mouth. Munching happily, he raised his fists over his head like Rocky on the steps of the Art Institute of Philadelphia. The crowd went bananas as the chefs quickly began assembling more salads. Soon each of the chefs had a plate, as did Deborah Hudson. More plates were piled with greens and fixings, and she started handing them into the crowd. Mackenzie and I snagged a plate and shared it.

Between bites, Mac said, "This definitely has to be the first course at our party, don't you think, P.C.?"

I was too busy chewing to answer her.

"Hey, don't hog it all!" Mac grabbed the plate away from me and scarfed down the rest of the salad.

When I looked up to see if there were any more plates coming around, I saw Billy Rose staggering around on stage, gripping his throat. Everyone cracked up at his antics, except for the other chefs, who looked annoyed. Suddenly, he dropped his fork and plate, leaned over, and started projectile vomiting all over the stage. Then Billy clutched his chest and fell to a crumpled heap.

Mackenzie whipped out her cell phone to call 911 as we ran up on stage. By the time we reached him, Billy's eyes were rolled up into his head, and he was making gagging sounds. Spittle flecked his lips. Not to mention other stuff.

"Mr. Rose!" I shouted at him. "Can you hear me?"

No response. I glanced at the shattered bowl of salad on the stage next to him, then turned to Deborah Hudson and yelled, "Get a doctor! Now!"

Not looking so mannequin-like anymore, Deborah clutched the microphone and croaked out, "Please, is there a doctor here? We need a doctor!"

The stage was suddenly swarming. Photographers' flashbulbs popped, and TV cameramen pushed their way forward trailing wires and cables. Everyone was shouting at each other and into cell phones. The audience was buzzing with confusion. Some people were screaming, some were crying. And in true New York fashion, a bunch of people rushed up to the foot of the stage to get in the best rubbernecking position as one of the stage crew knelt down next to Billy. He pinched his nose, and leaned down to puff air into his chest.

I grabbed the crewman's shoulder and pulled him away from Billy's face just as he was about to blow into his mouth. "Stop! Don't give him mouth-to-mouth!"

"What's the matter with you, kid?"

"It's too late for that," I said. "He's dead already. And if you put your mouth on his, you might end up dead too."

"What are you talking about, P.C.?" Mackenzie asked.

"He didn't choke on anything. It was the salad," I said. "Billy Rose was poisoned."

3

Parsley, Sage, Rosemary, and Crime

"Poisoned!" Deborah Hudson screeched. "Oh my God! Why is this happening to me?" Then she stumbled away, sobbing dramatically.

"Nice reaction," said Mackenzie. "P.C., are you sure?"

"Positive." I felt sick, as if I were going to engage in reverse peristalsis myself. We had just witnessed a cold-blooded murder.

Mackenzie whipped out the digital camera her mom had given her and started clicking. That was Mac—efficient, calm in a crisis, a great detective partner.

Seconds later an ambulance shrieked to a halt at the curb and three paramedics rushed up to the stage. One of the paramedics slipped an oxygen mask over Billy's face, while the other two started pounding his chest and giving his lifeless arm an injection. But nothing they did made any difference.

The chefs cowered in a corner of the stage in horror. Vladimira was saying, "It is terrible! Terrible!" to her bodyguard, who had joined her. Paul Zachary had turned a putrid shade of green, which showed up nicely against his ermine coat. Julius had collapsed into a chair, and was hyperventilating into a brown paper bag. His assistant, Robbie, who looked strangely serene, was hovering over him, trying to calm him down. And Danny Moran had his arms around Deborah Hudson and was patting her back while she clutched him with her dagger-like nails.

Three blue-and-white NYPD squad cars came screeching up the curb, lights flashing and sirens wailing. Half a dozen cops jumped out. "Off the stage! Clear out! Show's over!" the cops barked, clearing the festival photographers and cameramen off the stage. When they didn't move fast enough, the cops grabbed them and shoved them aside.

By this time, the paramedics had stopped working on Billy Rose. They covered his face with a sheet and started packing away their equipment. He was dead.

Twenty minutes later, the cops had questioned and released the celebrity chefs and their hangers-on. Mackenzie and I were still taking notes when a plain-clothes cop came over and introduced himself as Lieutenant Patrick Cooper. "Lady there says you think the man was poisoned," he said. "Isn't it more likely the guy had a heart attack or something?"

"Take a look," I said, pointing to Billy's spilled salad.

"Lettuce . . . croutons . . . looks like walnuts," said Lieutenant Cooper. "Nothing too remarkable. What are you getting at?"

Taking care not to touch anything, not wanting to disturb evidence, I knelt down and pointed at a deep-green, smooth, shiny leaf. It wasn't crinkly, or bright green, or tinged with purple like the other greens in the salad.

"See that dark green leaf that's not lettuce?"

"What is it, P.C.?" Mackenzie asked.

I stood up. "It's oleander. Genus *Nerium*, member of the dogbane family. A common ornamental shrub, found in backyards and gardens everywhere. Also found in decorative planters like those." I indicated the large planters placed around the stage. "It's highly toxic."

Lieutenant Cooper drew me and Mackenzie to the edge of the stage, away from where the other cops were taking statements from the stagehands and other witnesses.

"What are you, some kind of amateur horticulturalist?" said Lieutenant Cooper.

"Amateur detective, actually," I said. "Mackenzie and I both are. I don't know a lot about plants in general, but I do know a lot about poison. It's kind of a hobby of mine. Deadly nightshade, monkshood, locoweed— they're all common plants that'll kill you if you're stupid enough to take a bite out of them. But oleander is one of the deadliest substances you'll come into contact with in daily life."

"Is that so?" Lieutenant Cooper said. "And you say you're detectives?"

"We've helped out Lieutenant Krakowski on a couple

of cases," said Mackenzie. "One up at the Bronx Zoo, another at the Natural History Museum, where P.C.'s dad works. My mom is Kim Riggs—the City's chief medical examiner."

Lieutenant Cooper nodded. "And how do you know it wasn't an accident?"

"Oleander doesn't make its way into someone's salad by accident," I said.

Lieutenant Cooper gave Mackenzie and me a thoughtful look. "If you're right about that, we have a murder on our hands." He motioned to a couple of guys with nylon jackets that read NYPD—FORENSICS.

"I want that salad bagged," he told them. "It was the victim's last meal."

Turning back to Mackenzie and me, he asked, "Who made the salad?"

"All the chefs had a hand in it. Vladimira Koncharovna, Danny Moran, Paul Zachary, Julius LaCroix—each of them put an ingredient in the salad. And Deborah Hudson was the one who actually handed the plate to Billy Rose. The question is, who put in the oleander? And that, unfortunately, I didn't see."

"Were any of them acting strangely?" Lieutenant Cooper asked.

"I'd say they *all* were," Mackenzie said.

"How so?"

"Well, it was pretty obvious they can't stand one another," she said. "I mean, if looks could kill, we'd have four dead chefs onstage, not just one. But why was the one chef who didn't seem to be enemies with anyone the one who was killed? Does that make sense?"

"Poisoning someone in cold blood is senseless, Miss Riggs," said Lieutenant Cooper. Neither of us disagreed. He took down our names and phone numbers, and told us he'd probably need to ask us a few more questions later.

The crime scene had been cordoned off by the uniformed cops, and Deborah Hudson and the celebrity chefs were nowhere to be seen. But we saw that the coroner's van had arrived. Mac craned her neck to see who was driving it. "P.C., there's Dave Wisner, my mom's assistant," she said. "Dave!" she called, waving to the rotund, balding man who got out of the van.

"Mackenzie?" he said, peering up at her through his thick glasses. "What are you doing here?"

"We saw it happen!" said Mac. "A man died—was murdered—right before our eyes! It was horrible!"

"Now, now, let's not jump to conclusions," said Dave. "Death could have been caused by stroke, heart attack, any number of—"

"He was poisoned," I said. "Oleander. I'm sure of it. Check it out."

Mackenzie and I led Dave over to where Billy lay, surrounded by cops. The cops parted to let him through. Dave snapped on a pair of gloves and knelt down to examine the body.

A few minutes later, he stood up, ripped off his gloves, and led us over to Lieutenant Cooper, who was still taking notes on the scene. "I'll have to wait till toxicology provides a final report on the blood and saliva samples," he said, polishing his glasses on his shirttail. "But judging from the swelling of the throat and eyeballs, and from the characteristic blue pallor of the dermis, I'd say Mackenzie and her friend here are right. The victim was poisoned."

4

Hate at First Bite

At that, Mackenzie said good-bye to Dave, grabbed my arm, and practically dragged me off the stage. "C'mon, P.C., let's get out of here."

"What's the rush, Mackenzie?" I asked as we made our way through the thinning crowd toward Fifth Avenue.

"I wanted to beat it before you got it into that lame brain of yours that we should get involved the case."

"Me?" I asked, pressing my hand to my chest. "Why would you think I'd get mixed up in a murder investigation? And anyway, who was it taking pictures of the crime scene?"

"Don't make me haul off and whomp you, P.C.," said Mackenzie. "I was taking those snaps just in case the police missed something. But we've got enough on our plate without trying to figure out who poisoned Billy Rose's salad. Our party, remember?"

"Aha!" I said, baiting the hook. "That's the thing. Whoever put those oleander leaves in the salad wasn't intending to poison Billy Rose. They were meant for Julius LaCroix."

Mackenzie stopped dead in her tracks. "I think you're right," she said, after a minute. "Billy couldn't have been the intended victim."

"But he got it nevertheless," I said, reeling her in. "How sad. It's bad enough to die so young, but to be the accidental victim of a murder attempt gone wrong. . . . Poor Billy Rose. A rising star, liked by everyone, with such potential. He had so much to live for."

If Mackenzie had been a trout, she'd have been in the net.

"P.C., I just thought of something," she said, clutching my arm. "If that salad was meant for Julius LaCroix, it means there's someone still out there who wants him dead."

We'd come down Fifth Avenue as far as Fifty-first Street and were now standing in front of St. Patrick's Cathedral. A large stage had been erected on the front steps for the food festival. Poles with klieg lights, tall booms with microphones, and camera dollies bristled around the set. The set itself was essentially a full gourmet kitchen, with a twelve-foot granite countertop, Sub-Zero fridge, and an eight-burner Viking range.

A large banner at the back read THE GOURMET ZONE, WITH CHEF JULIUS LACROIX OF RESTAURANT L'AVENTURE. Julius's olive-green Hummer was parked down the block next to a trailer, so we knew he—and Robbie McGrath—must be around. A large sandwich board on the sidewalk in front of the stage read

COME SEE CHEF JULIUS PERFORM LIVE, 4 P.M., SUNDAY, MARCH 28.

"That's tomorrow," I said.

"The filming of Julius's TV show is the highlight of the festival every year," said Mackenzie. "I've had it programmed into my Palm Pilot since last year. I wouldn't miss it for anything."

"Neither would Julius, I'm sure," I said. "Unless he doesn't live long enough."

"We've got to warn him," said Mackenzie. "But how do we find him?"

"Let's see if there's anyone here who can help us get a hold of him."

On the edge of the set we spotted Robbie. He was talking to a woman with a clipboard, who in turn was directing techies to adjust lights and microphones. We went up to him and introduced ourselves.

"You must be Julius LaCroix's assistant," I said. "We saw you with him just now."

"Yes, I remember you two. I gave Mrs. Lester your passes, in fact. My official title is Executive Advocate-in-Confidence, Director of Endeavor Coordination," Robbie said. "But yes, I am his personal assistant. What can I do for you?"

"We need to talk to Mr. LaCroix about what happened to Billy Rose," I said. "He was murdered—poisoned."

Without skipping a beat, Robbie waved to the woman

who was directing the workers onstage and said, "I'm taking five, Marjorie." I was surprised at his lack of surprise and I remembered his strongly calm reaction to Billy's gruesome demise. He drew us aside. "It's a tragedy. Simply a tragedy. That poor kid. So much talent, snuffed out so suddenly! Julius was terribly, terribly upset."

"I'm sure you must be, too," said Mackenzie, pointedly. "Everyone who saw it happen is."

"Yes, well. *Que será, será,* as the song goes."

I felt like slapping his face with a paddleball—just to see if I'd get a reaction. I could see from Mac's face that she felt the same way.

"We need to talk to Mr. LaCroix about why someone would want to kill him," Mackenzie said.

"Kill Julius?" said Robbie, sounding shocked. Finally, some emotion. For a minute there, he reminded me of Mr. Data, the android on *Star Trek: The Next Generation.*

"Yes," I said. "We don't think Billy was the intended victim."

"What do you mean?" said Robbie.

"We think someone was trying to kill Mr. LaCroix," Mackenzie said. "Deborah Hudson had announced that he would eat that salad. It was only by sheer luck that he didn't. And we're afraid that since the murderer failed the first time, he might try again. The chef needs to know he's in danger."

"Oh dear," Robbie said. "I'd better tell Julius right away."

Mac and I nodded enthusiastically.

"Yes!" Mackenzie said. "And we would very, very much like to speak with him ourselves."

"Sorry, kids," Robbie said, shaking his head. He started walking toward the Hummer and the trailer. We followed. "I'm afraid that won't be possible. Mr. LaCroix is extremely upset now, he has a busy day tomorrow, and he needs his rest. I'll be certain to tell him what you told me, but for now I'm afraid I can't allow you to—"

"Please, Mr. McGrath," Mackenzie said, raising her voice. "Mr. LaCroix might be able to shed some light on who might have wanted to kill him. We need to speak to him."

"Young lady, lower your voice! How dare—"

Julius LaCroix came out of the trailer. "What did these young people wish to talk to me about?"

Quickly, over Robbie's loud objections, Mackenzie and I explained the reasoning behind our belief that he, Julius, had been the intended recipient of the fatal salad.

"Dear me!" said Julius. "But why would anyone want to kill me?" His face had gone gray, and his eyes darted about nervously.

Neither Mackenzie, nor I, nor Robbie McGrath ventured an answer to that one. The question was left hanging in the air.

"You might want to go to the police and ask for protection," I suggested.

Julius didn't seem to hear me. He just stared off into space, like his mind had gone on a vacation. I felt terrible. He was tall, over six feet, but now he seemed all shriveled up, defeated.

Robbie took charge. "Thank you for your concern," he said. "But we'll handle it. Now, good-bye!" He maneuvered Julius through the trailer door.

"We'd like to talk to you about—" I tried to say, but Robbie cut me off.

"Don't you think you've done enough? He can't talk to you, he's too upset." And he slammed the trailer door before I could get another word in.

What could we do? We'd done our duty by warning Julius, so we decided to leave him and Robbie in peace—for the time being.

Mackenzie and I meandered further down Fifth Avenue, hashing over Julius's unwillingness to talk to us further. "He seemed almost scared of us," Mac said.

"Well, it's understandable," I said. "He must be freaking out, knowing that someone just tried to kill him. And he doesn't know us from Adam and Eve. For all he knows, we were the ones who put that oleander in the salad."

"I guess," said Mackenzie doubtfully. "But I got the feeling he was scared for some other reason. My scalp was tingling like crazy."

Mackenzie's practically a human lie detector. When the top of her head tingles, it means something is not kosher.

Fifth Avenue had been blocked off to vehicular traffic from Fifty-ninth Street all the way down to Forty-second, where the festival had its storefront headquarters in the former location of an old-fashioned delicatessan. Over the picture windows was a big neon sign that still read BLATTBERG'S in red art deco script. Underneath was a more modern-looking sign that read HOME OF THE NEW YORK IS FOOD COUNTRY FESTIVAL.

"Should we go in and see if we can catch Deborah Hudson?" I asked. "After all, she was the last one before Billy to touch the salad. Maybe she saw something suspicious."

"Or did something suspicious," Mackenzie said. "Let's not cross her off the list of suspects yet. Just because she's blond and pretty doesn't mean she couldn't be a cold-blooded killer, P.C."

Walking into Blattberg's Deli was like entering a time warp. Even though the place was no longer a functioning deli, the food festival staff who now used it as an office had redecorated as little as possible. Strung from the ceiling were yellowing signs of Second World War vintage that read SEND A SALAMI TO YOUR BOY IN THE ARMY. The smell of pastrami and pickles still permeated the air.

Holding court in the center of the room was Deborah Hudson. We were about to go up to her when Danny Moran walked in and brushed right by us.

"Hey, babe," he said, "you okay now?"

"God, Danny, am I glad to see you. This place is a madhouse. The phones are ringing off the hook," she wailed.

Danny drew her aside, and they huddled together at the back of the room. We couldn't hear what they were saying, but it looked like she was about to go into hysterical freak-out mode again. We caught snatches of things like "ex-husband" and "gloating" and a few unmentionable four-letter words.

"Whaddaya say we go break up the lovebirds?" said Mackenzie.

"You think we should?"

She got a mischievous glint in her eye. "Yeah, sure. One of them might be a murderer, you know. Maybe even both of them."

Mackenzie crossed the room, with me right behind her. A junior-executive type, in pressed Oxford-cloth shirt, power-yellow tie, and tasseled loafers, tried to stop her, but Mackenzie barreled straight past him like Jerome Bettis through the Cincinnati Bengals' defensive line.

"Ms. Hudson," Mackenzie said, breaking into the clear, "could we speak to you for a minute, please?"

Deborah seemed startled to see us. "Excuse me?"

"Could we speak to you about what happened to Billy Rose? We're investigating his murder."

Deborah sighed dramatically and turned to Danny. "See? It's starting already. I'll talk to you later."

Danny nodded. "Sure thing, babe. I gotta get back to the restaurant. Big crowd tonight." He winked at her and walked off, whistling. He seemed a little too cheerful for someone who had just witnessed a murder. I made a mental note to check him out later.

With Danny gone, Deborah made an effort to pull herself together. She turned to Mackenzie, in all-business mode again. "How may I help you?"

"My name's Mackenzie Riggs, and this is my friend P.C. Hawke."

"Yes, I remember you two," Deborah said. She turned to me. "You're the one who said Billy was poisoned."

"Yes. Any idea who might have done it?"

I paused, observing Deborah closely, seeing if she would give anything away. Would she look away guiltily, or flush red, or fiddle with her hands? But no. She didn't show any of the telltale signs of someone who was trying to hide something.

"I have no idea."

"Did you notice anything suspicious? Anything out of the ordinary?" Mackenzie asked.

Deborah's cell phone chirped, and she took a moment to field the call. Then: "Not really. It was just business as usual with the five hottest chefs in New York all together on stage. An all-out cat fight."

"What do you mean?" Mackenzie asked.

"Listen, kids. Cooking is an art, not a science. Any chef worth his salt—no pun intended—is an artist.

They're creative, unpredictable. Impulsive. Top-flight chefs are like rock stars."

"They've even got groupies," I said.

"Well, yes. They do. There's something terribly seductive about a well-made soufflé." Deborah put away her cell phone so she could dish the dirt undisturbed. "They've got colossal egos. Each is accustomed to being master of the kitchen, the absolute ruler of his or her domain. The star of the show. And they don't like to share the spotlight."

"And Julius LaCroix—he's number one, right?" I said.

Deborah nodded. "For years he's been the critics' darling. Every year *Gotham Gourmet* magazine uses the food festival to reassess its top-ten list. Whoever the *Gourmet* anoints number one can basically do no wrong—and the rest of the press, including the *New York Times*, *New York* magazine, and all the other heavy hitters, follow suit."

"I had no idea the *Gotham Gourmet* was so influential," said Mackenzie.

"Believe it. And being named top chef in the city can mean a couple million dollars in extra revenue for the chef's restaurant," said Deborah. "Even the number-two spot is worth a million. Julius has been number one for so long, he's thinks he's the Pope—like he's got a lifelong appointment. But there's been talk that Julius is slipping. His ratings for his TV show are down. People say that the quality of presentation at L'Aventure has fallen a notch. Everyone thinks that this is the year that Paul Zachary, the Susan Lucci of the New York restaurant scene, might finally take home the big prize."

Just then a gofer came up with a pink "While You Were Away" slip and said to Deborah, "Julius LaCroix just called. Said he has a doctor's appointment tomorrow at noon, so his preshow interviews and so forth will have to be scheduled around that. Here's his number if you need it." He handed Deborah the slip of paper and left.

"Doctor's appointment at noon?" I said. "They go on air live at four. With makeup and rehearsals isn't that cutting it a little close?"

"Julius is getting older," Deborah said. "He's had heart problems. We'll just have to work around the doctor's appointment. It's just one more of a million things I'm dealing with."

"Is there anything else you can tell us about the chefs?" Mackenzie asked.

Deborah thought for a moment, then said, "Why don't I give you a copy of our book? There's one right here." She walked behind a glassed-in counter and pulled out a book entitled *Come Fry with Me—Signature Dishes of the Top New York Chefs*. "Julius *persuaded* the festival to buy five thousand copies and give them out as promotional items," she said. I picked up on the sarcasm in her tone.

"Persuaded?" I repeated.

"He said he wouldn't participate in the festival if we didn't take the five thousand," Deborah explained. "We need him as much as he needs us, so in the end we took it. The book was compiled by his protégé, Robbie McGrath. Maybe you've met him?"

"We just did," I said.

"You seem like a good judge of people, Ms. Hudson," said Mackenzie, buttering her up. "What do you think of Robbie McGrath?"

"He's very supportive of Julius," she said.

I decided to take a gamble. "That salad wasn't meant for Billy Rose, you know. Whoever put poison in it was gunning for Julius."

Deborah looked shocked. "You're not implying Robbie McGrath tried to kill Julius, are you?"

"Not at all," I said. "Right now we don't know who the murderer is. But I'm wondering who would gain by Julius's death."

"Well, everyone knows that Robbie is Julius's heir apparent," said Deborah. "Since Julius never had any children, it's widely assumed that Robbie will inherit his estate."

"Really?" Mackenzie said. "We'll keep that in mind."

"Of course, Robbie isn't the only one who would stand to gain from Julius's demise." Deborah seemed to be enjoying herself now. "There's Paul Zachary. No more Julius LaCroix, and Paul would be the undisputed king of New York chefs. And they've despised each other for so long, it wouldn't surprise me at all if Paul was the culprit. Speaking of which, I have to get back to work." She took her cell phone out of her pocket and turned it back on. Immediately it chirped. "You can see it's a circus around here."

"We understand," said Mackenzie. "Thanks for taking the time to talk with us."

"Sure thing." She shook our hands quickly, then said, "Deborah here," into the phone.

Back out on the street, we decided to do a little more snooping.

"We've got to check out Paul Zachary," I said. "He had the motive and the opportunity."

"Okay," Mackenzie agreed, "but I wouldn't forget about Deborah Hudson too quickly. Her boyfriend-chef Danny would move up a notch too if Julius bit the dust. And she strikes me as having a heart like iceberg lettuce."

5

Stir-Fried Crazy

"So where do things stand now?" I asked Mackenzie.

"Well, since Billy was a young guy, just starting out, he hadn't made enemies the way the older chefs had," said Mackenzie.

"And it seems like everyone except Robbie hates Julius," I said. "Since the salad was supposed to be for him, he must have been the intended victim."

"On the other hand, it was Deborah Hudson who actually put the plate into Billy's hands," Mackenzie pointed out. "So if she's the murderer, then Billy really was the intended victim. But why would Deborah want to kill Billy?"

I shrugged. "Search me. It seems more likely that it was someone trying to kill Julius, and Billy just got unlucky. And Paul Zachary would have the most to gain from Julius's death."

Mackenzie flipped to the festival schedule of events printed in the *Gotham Gourmet*. "It says here that Paul Zachary is going to do a presentation at his restaurant at three," she said. "What time is it now?"

"Five of."

"Let's get going then."

We arrived at The Season of the Dove just as Paul Zachary was finishing up his presentation. He had taken off his fur coat but not his purple glasses. In his sparkly, rhinestone-studded white chef's outfit, he looked like a thin Elvis, the Later Years. A sort of portable kitchen, similar to the one Julius would be filming from tomorrow but considerably smaller, had been set up in front of the restaurant.

"And *voilà*!" Paul announced to the fifty or so spectators gathered around his stage. "Out comes the squab, baked to perfection. Inside is the exquisite foie gras. And on top we pour the delicious white-truffle sauce. Don't worry, my little friend," he said, addressing the dead pigeon on the platter before him, "this will only tickle a little bit."

The crowd laughed at Zachary's antics as he doused the bird in a rich, creamy sauce. "Tee-hee-hee, that feels so good!" he said, speaking for the squab. "And now, samples for everyone!" A dozen aproned assistants materialized out of the restaurant, bearing trays loaded with more of Zachary's signature dish.

"Oooh, let's grab a taste," said Mackenzie.

"Um, Miss Vegetarian-Wanna-Be, isn't foie gras just another name for goose-liver sausage? So that would appear to be a bird stuffed with another bird's liver," I pointed out.

"P.C., this is a once-in-a-lifetime opportunity!" she said. "A dish like this could *make* our party." She looked starry-eyed at the thought.

I had to snap her out of it. Her bizarrely uncharacteristic social-climbing was beginning to scare me. "Mackenzie, do you realize that Paul Zachary's foie gras comes from geese specially bred and raised on his personal farm in France? The birds are kept immobilized and are force-fed grain to fatten up their livers."

"Oh, ick! Where'd you hear that?"

"*Gotham Gourmet*. And do you know just how they force-feed them?"

"Don't tell me . . ."

"A funnel down their throats!"

"Okay, P.C. I get the point. Now shut up."

"Let's go grill Paul Zachary," I said, leading the way.

Paul Zachary had retreated to the front doors of the restaurant, where he stood watching the crowd sample his creation.

"Mr. Zachary," I said, approaching him, but one of his assistants stepped between the chef and me.

"Mr. Zachary isn't handing out autographs," he said, folding his arms across his chest in a don't-mess-with-me-pipsqueak stance.

"We're not looking for an autograph," I explained. "We wanted to talk to him about Billy Rose. We have some important information regard—"

"Take a hike, kid," the guy said, taking a step toward me.

But Zachary said, "It's all right, let the children in."

The guy finally stepped aside, glaring at me as I passed.

Inside, The Season of the Dove was all dark wood and muted tones, with burgundy cloths on the tables and smoky old oil paintings on the walls. The decor said three things: money, money, and money.

"Is it true that Billy Rose was poisoned," Zachary said, coming straight to the point.

"That's what the coroner thinks. He had swallowed a lot of oleander," I said. "And it's hard to explain how oleander could have wound up in that salad unless someone put it there on purpose."

"How dreadful!" Zachary tsk-tsked. "Who could have done such a thing?"

"That's just it, Mr. Zachary," said Mackenzie. "We don't believe anyone did want him dead. That salad, remember, was made to order for Julius LaCroix. The question is, Who would want Julius LaCroix dead?"

"Goodness, I couldn't possibly imagine who would want to harm dear old Julius," said Zachary.

Now, Mackenzie's the one with the scalp that goes tingly when someone's feeding her a line. I'm normally not nearly so sensitive to the psychological nuances between people. I'm better with the logical stuff. But even my lie detector was buzzing like crazy over Zachary's "dear old Julius" baloney.

"It's true, Julius and I have been competitors for

years," he went on. "I never minded all the times he 'borrowed' my recipes or lured away my bartenders, waiters, and cooks. Goodness, no!"

I bet not, I said to myself, and glanced at Mackenzie. She reached up casually and gave her head a little scratch. That was her signal to me that she thought Zachary was full of boo-yah.

"Despite all that, we've shared nothing but respect and affection," Zachary went on. "I like to think we spurred each other to ever greater heights of culinary accomplishment. In fact, I've always defended Julius against colleagues like Vladimira Koncharovna and that vulgarian Danny Moran who spread gossip that Julius is backbiting me."

"You don't say," I commented.

"I do say!" said Zachary. "Now, even though Julius and I are practically like brothers, there are other people who would love to see him take a fall. I'm not one to spread gossip. . . ."

"Naturally," said Mackenzie.

"But Julius has made his fair share of enemies," said Zachary. "Why, if I weren't as forgiving and understanding as I am, even *I* might resent him. Did you know he had a clause put into his *Gourmet Zone* TV contract that said the network couldn't hire any other New York chef as long as his show is on the air?"

"Is that legal?" Mackenzie asked.

"Legal, shmegal," said Zachary. "What can you do?

Now, I'm sure he didn't mean to hurt my or anyone else's business. But some others aren't so forgiving. They say Julius is devious and unethical, but I try not to listen to them."

"Certainly not," I said, adding silently, You just repeat everything they say.

"I hear the quality of Julius's food at L'Aventure has gone downhill faster than Robert Redford skiing off a cliff at Sundance," he said, really getting into it now. His chunky gold pinky ring clattered against the table as he waved his hands about. "Some people say such cruel things. I know for a fact that Julius used to make everything from scratch—it was nouvelle cuisine at its finest. Now there are gossipmongers who say he buys his chocolate mousse from Sara Lee and his quiche Lorraine from Costco."

"Really?" Mackenzie said, pretending to be scandalized.

"People are so unkind, don't you think?" Zachary was so catty, he was going to need to be fitted for a flea collar. "Some of his critics even say that ever since he's had heart problems, it's like the blood isn't getting to his brain. They say he's become a culinary fraud. Isn't that vicious of them?"

"What about his signature dish, crawfish pie?" Mackenzie asked. "I read that the critics say that one bite of Julius LaCroix's crawfish pie makes the whole world seems like a friendlier place."

"It's still satisfactory," Zachary admitted. He said *satisfactory* as if he meant "totally unacceptable." "He serves it with a side of dirty rice and a daringly common fruit salad."

"Sounds delicious," I said, just to goad him further.

"Hmph," Zachary said. He plucked at the ruffles on his shirt front. "I'll never understand that man's appeal. And now they say Ronald Crumfeld's going to put him in charge of his newest restaurant, Willow at the Edge of the Forest."

"Ronald Crumfeld?" I said. "He's that big developer guy, right?"

"He owns half of Brooklyn, my dear boy. And now he's going uptown—putting up a high-rise on Fifty-seventh Street. Very chichi. Willow at the Edge of the Forest will be on the top floor—the most prestigious address in the whole city. It's simply inexplicable that that fraud, that *charlatan*, will be heading it up!"

Zachary was practically seething with jealousy by now. And too far gone to hide it.

"You know," he went on, "you two might want to talk to that hideous Robbie McGrath creature. Other people—people more unfeeling than I, of course—have questioned his peculiar devotion to Julius. What's in it for Robbie? As for Julius, they say it's only Robbie's cookbook that keeps alive the utter fiction that Julius is the number-one chef in the City."

"We'll keep that in mind when we talk to Robbie again," I said.

"I'd be careful if I were you," said Zachary. "With Robbie, and with everyone else. If someone's really out to kill Julius, they're not going to appreciate your snooping around."

"We'll keep that in mind too," I said.

We thanked Zachary for taking the time to talk with us.

"By the way, I adore your Hello Kitty hair clip," he said to Mackenzie.

"Thanks," she said. "Two ninety-eight, at Screaming Mimi's."

"I'll remember that."

6

The Long Hot Simmer

"**Where to now?**" Mackenzie asked.

"Oddly enough," I said, "I'm kind of hungry. Famished, actually."

"Let's head back to the festival, then," said Mackenzie. "Maybe there'll be some broiled snails or raw oysters for you to snack on."

"Gosh, maybe. Or maybe we could just drop into the coffee shop on the corner over there so I could get some real food—a BLT on rye and a chocolate egg cream."

"Whatever you say. You're sure you don't want snails, though?"

"Positive."

We went into the Pillars of Athens coffee shop and put in an order to go.

"Let's call Jesus," I said. "Maybe he can dig up more info on our suspects."

Jesus Lopez is a friend of ours who's one of the all-time greatest hackers. Computers at the Pentagon, the CIA, you name it, and he's hacked into it. He's even reached the Holy Grail of hackerdom—the mainframe at George Lucas's Skywalker ranch. Jesus is the only non-Lucas employee on earth to already have seen footage from the next *Star Wars* movie.

"Jesus?" I said into my cell phone. "Mackenzie and I need your help."

"What's the problem, buddy?"

I explained. "Can you do us a favor?"

"Sure, man. My pleasure."

"Find anything you can about the victim, Billy Rose. Also Vladimira Koncharovna, Danny Moran, and Paul Zachary. We think one of them might be trying to kill Julius LaCroix. And check out Julius, too."

"Not a problem. A little surfing ought to bag me plenty of info. Anything else?"

"See if anything unusual on any of them pops out at you—tax returns, criminal records, that kind of thing."

"Check out their taxes? That means hacking into the IRS."

"If you're going to do anything illegal, don't tell me about it," I said.

Jesus laughed. "Illegal? Me? Never!"

"Okay, Jesus," I said. "And hey, thanks, man."

"Catch you later, dude."

I put away the cell phone, and Mackenzie said, "When that BLT comes, can I have a bite?"

"I knew you were going to say that." I paid the man behind the counter for the sandwich and egg cream, and we set off west, back toward Fifth Avenue.

"According to the schedule, Julius himself is going to be performing in half an hour at his set on the steps of St. Patrick's. It's a warm-up for tomorrow's big TV show."

A few minutes later we were back in front of the *Gourmet Zone* set, where Julius LaCroix had just taken the stage. He was showing the crowd how to prepare chicken with raspberry-vinegar sauce. As opposed to Paul Zachary, who dressed flamboyantly and clowned around playing for laughs, Julius presented a more dignified, restrained style. His soothing voice was almost hypnotic.

"We sauté the breasts in clarified butter," Julius said. "You make clarified butter, by the way, by melting butter and then spooning out the white globs of milk solids. What you're left with is clear, golden, *clarified* butter."

Julius went on like this for another couple of minutes, explaining in a friendly, comforting way his technique for cooking the perfect bird. The audience loved it. Even I had to admit he was oddly compelling—he had an undeniable charisma, with his deep voice and shock of white hair—and I don't make a habit of watching cooking shows.

I looked around. There were two uniformed cops on each side of the stage, plus three in the front row of spectators. Several more husky guys in trench coats, with wires coming out of their ears, were stationed around the stage—obviously plainclothes officers. We waved to Lieutenant Cooper, who was standing downstage. He nodded back.

"I have a bad feeling about this," I said to Mackenzie. "If someone's out to get Julius, the last thing he should be doing is making public appearances."

"I know," said Mackenzie. "The top of my head's tingling like crazy. That's always a sign of trouble. But at least the lieutenant is doing a good job with the police presence."

Now that we were up on the stage, I could see over the sea of faces watching Julius perform. I scanned the audience for familiar faces.

"Look," I said to Mackenzie, nudging her. "Here comes Zachary in his pink Caddy."

Paul Zachary, now dressed in a floor-length chartreuse duster and ten-gallon hat, joined Vladimira Koncharovna at the back of the crowd. We were too far away to hear anything they were saying, especially since they were huddling together conspiratorially.

"Not exactly the most inconspicuous of entrances," Mackenzie said. "I wonder what brings him here."

"And what they're doing together, considering all that hostility between them," I said.

"Maybe it's a case of 'the enemy of my enemy is my friend.'"

At the front of the stage, Julius said, "Now I'll demonstrate my method for creating the perfect chocolate raspberry torte, to go with the raspberry-vinegar chickens."

The odor of baking chicken filled the air as Julius arranged a bowl full of raspberries, a plate of butter, several other bowls and plates, and a couple of decorative canisters on the granite countertop.

"First we make the filling," he said, dumping the raspberries into a mixing bowl. Then he added lemon juice, a dollop of whipped cream, and sugar from one of the canisters.

While he mixed and mashed, he chatted amiably with the audience. "Chocolate and raspberries—what could be more delicious? Chocolate was unknown to Europeans before the discovery of the Americas, you know."

Setting aside the raspberries, he got out another mixing bowl and measured out some butter, flour, and sugar, and added three eggs for the cake. Mixing and mashing, he said, "To the ancient Maya, chocolate was the drink of gods and poets. How true!"

The audience laughed and clapped.

"Money talks. Chocolate sings," he quipped. "And now to make the chocolate sauce. We take two cups of boiling water . . ."

Moving discreetly onstage, Robbie handed him a saucepan he'd set on the stove a few minutes earlier and poured the hot water into a mixing bowl. "We mix in two cups of the finest grade powdered cocoa from Belgium."

With a flourish, Julius pried the top off one of the decorative tin canisters. He glanced inside and did a brief double take. For a moment, he looked frozen. He had a weird twitchy look on his face, like a rabbit in the headlights. Then he pulled something out of the canister, stuffed it into his trousers pockets, and continued with his banter.

"Did you see that?" I whispered to Mackenzie.

"Yes," she said. "It looked like there was a piece of paper in there."

"You know, if you can't eat all your chocolate, you can keep it in the freezer," Julius said, reaching into the canister again, this time with a measuring cup. He dug with the cup into the cocoa. "But if you can't eat all your chocolate, what's wrong with you?"

As the crowd chuckled at his witticism, Julius dug into the canister again for the second cup of cocoa, then suddenly yanked his hand out and screamed. The canister flew out of his hands and clattered up against the back wall of the set in a brown cloud of cocoa powder.

"A scorpion!" Julius cried, clutching the hand that had been in the canister. "A scorpion!"

A large black scorpion, with its evil-looking hooked tail, scuttled out of the pile of cocoa on the floor of the set.

There are only two bugs I don't like: cockroaches and scorpions. Cockroaches are unavoidable in New York City, so you almost have to get used to them. But scorpions . . . ugh!

Quick as a flash, Lieutenant Cooper rushed forward, grabbed an empty glass bowl from the countertop, and raced to the back of the set. He slammed the bowl down over the scorpion so that it was trapped, unharmed, inside. The creepy bug skittered frantically around underneath the glass, searching for an exit, its tail raised high in a posture that said "Don't mess with me unless you want a taste of this."

Julius, meanwhile, had dropped to his knees in the middle of the stage, rocking back and forth, cradling his hands. Four uniformed cops had surrounded him. Robbie McGrath was, of course, at Julius's side.

I looked out into the panic-stricken crowd, which was abuzz with fear and curiosity. "Where's Zachary?" I asked Mackenzie. "I don't see him."

"Me neither," she said. "Looks like he saw what he'd come to see."

The cops had hustled Julius to the back of the stage, where a doctor was checking his blood pressure. Lieutenant Cooper barked into his cell phone, "Give me the entomology department at the Natural History Museum," he said.

"Ask for Dr. Skinner," I said, coming up to the lieutenant. "She's the world's foremost authority on scorpions."

"How did you know that?" Lieutenant Cooper asked.

"My dad works at the museum," I said.

Lieutenant Cooper soon had Dr. Skinner on the line. "It's black, about two and a half inches long. . . . That's right. . . . No, no stripes or other markings. Solid black. . . . That's a relief. Thank you, Dr. Skinner."

"What'd she say?" I asked after he'd hung up.

Lieutenant Cooper walked with me and Mackenzie over to where Julius sat slumped in a chair, looking like a man who was preparing to have a nice big coronary. His face was the color of boiled liver.

"I just spoke to an expert on scorpions, Mr. LaCroix," said Lieutenant Cooper. "She was sure from my description that we're dealing with one of the less deadly varieties of scorpion. She assured me that the sting is no worse than a bee sting. She recommends you take some aspirin for the swelling, but other than that, you won't be in need of medical treatment."

"Thank God!" said Robbie. "You're sure we won't need to go to the hospital?"

"It's what the doctor said."

Julius just sat expressionlessly in his chair.

"Mr. LaCroix, if you don't mind my asking," I said, "what was it you found in the canister of cocoa, before you found the scorpion? It looked like some kind of note."

"Huh?" He gazed up at me, a wonky expression on his face. "Oh, just an inspection slip, from the canister's manufacturer. Number twelve gave it a pass. I threw the slip away. Please, I'm very tired now. My hand hurts, and I have a doctor's appointment I'm already late for."

"We're on our way, Julius," said Robbie. "I've called for the car. We'll be at the doctor's in no time."

"I'll have a squad car accompany you," Lieutenant Cooper said.

"That won't be necessary, Lieutenant," said Robbie. "I'm sure we can manage."

"Suit yourself," said Lieutenant Cooper.

We walked with him to the edge of the stage, while Robbie helped Julius down the steps to where their green Hummer was waiting for them.

"If you ask me," said Mackenzie to Lieutenant Cooper and me as we watched Robbie and Julius drive off, "Julius was lying about that being an inspection slip in the canister. From the look on his face, I'd say it was one scary recipe."

"Take her word for it," I said. "Mackenzie can always tell when someone's lying."

Lieutenant Cooper nodded but didn't say anything. He was a man of few words, but the words he did say counted.

We thanked Lieutenant Cooper again, and climbed down from the stage to head back up Fifth Avenue. As we got to Fifty-third Street, I recognized a familiar car halfway up the block.

"There's Paul Zachary's car," I said pointing. Zachary himself was just climbing behind the wheel. "Let's go ask him why he was hanging around Julius's show."

We started trotting down the sidewalk toward him, and called out, "Mr. Zachary! Mr. Zachary, wait!"

But the big pink Caddy squealed out from the curb. Zachary never even looked back.

7

Out of the Frying Pan

"He's probably heading back to The Season of the Dove," I said.

"Let's go over there," said Mackenzie. "I want to talk with him. I'm sure he heard us calling for him, and he took off on purpose. What's his deal?"

"Whatever his deal is, it smells fishy," I said. "Just like his cooking."

"Say what you will about Paul Zachary, P.C. He may be a liar, a blackmailer, or a cold-blooded killer for all we know. But he's a heckuva cook."

"If you like that sort of thing," I said.

The sun was dipping down below the skyscrapers that lined Sixth Avenue, casting long shadows as we walked east on Fifty-third Street. A sudden chill had come over the air. The midtown streets were eerily quiet. It seemed strange to be walking down sidewalks that were usually packed with people but were now completely deserted. A shredded plastic shopping bag whirled in lonely circles in a grimy doorway. In the distance a car alarm squealed.

"I'm getting the creeps," Mackenzie said, as we got to the corner of Park Avenue. "Let's hail a cab and get out of here."

"Wait," I said. "Look there. Zachary's car."

The gaudy pink Caddy was parked in front of North-Astor's, the giant eight-story department store that takes up an entire city block at Fifty-ninth and Lex.

"Why would he be going into North-Astor's now?" I said.

"Well, they carry his line of cookware," Mackenzie said. "Maybe he's checking to make sure it's in stock. Or maybe he's going to sign autographs."

"Let's tail him, see what he's up to."

We approached the bank of revolving doors in front. A sign posted on one of the doors said the store closed at seven P.M. on Saturdays. I checked my watch. Ten of. A few frazzled-looking customers straggled out the doors. No one but Mackenzie and me was going in.

"Ah, eau de department store," I said as we entered the building. "Stale perfume, new carpet, and floor wax."

"Zachary's not going to get away from us this time," Mackenzie said. "Look, there he is, heading for the escalator."

In his big hat and long green coat, Zachary was hardly a difficult figure to spot. He was on the down escalator, which led to North-Astor's basement, a whole floor devoted to gourmet foods and high-end kitchen equipment.

We followed him down, taking care to stay out of

sight. We stepped off the escalator and scurried behind a display of fancy tea kettles. We heard a sales clerk greet him by name. "Why, hello, Mr. Zachary. Can I help you with anything?"

"He must come here often, for the clerk to recognize him like that," I whispered to Mackenzie.

"No, thank you, Stephen," said Zachary. "I'm merely browsing."

"I'm locking up the register now," said Stephen. "The store will be closing in two minutes. If you want to purchase anything, you'll have to take it to the main register on the first floor."

"Very well," said Zachary. "Thank you, dear boy. And you have a splendid evening."

"I will, sir," said Stephen. We watched him go up the escalator.

We were now alone with Zachary in the basement. He wasn't aware we were there, and we moved silently down the aisles, tracking him as he hummed quietly to himself. Occasionally he would pick an item off a shelf, examine it absentmindedly, and put it back.

"What's he up to?" I whispered to Mackenzie. "Didn't he hear the man? The store's closing."

"It's almost like he's waiting for something," Mackenzie said. "Or someone."

Suddenly the main overhead lights went out. The only illumination came from small lamps inset in the ceiling about every thirty feet—enough light to keep you from walking headlong into a display case, but not enough to do much else. A voice came over the P.A. system, announcing, "Attention, shoppers. North-Astor's is now closed. Please take your merchandise to the front of the store. Thank you."

In the dim half-light the kitchen gadgets took on a sinister aspect. Knives set up in neat rows in glass cases glinted dully.

"I don't like the looks of this," Mackenzie muttered.

A row of heavy-duty mixers, their hinged heads set back like yawning animals with vicious-looking mouths, lined a nearby shelf. Fancy ergonomic corkscrews, can openers, and potato mashers looked like inscrutable instruments of medieval torture.

"I don't like it either," I said. "Maybe we should get out of here."

The potential uses to which the array of ice picks could be put became suddenly apparent.

"P.C.!" Mackenzie whispered. "Where did Zachary go?"

We froze, listening intently for some sign of his whereabouts.

"Don't know," I said.

The creak and whir of elevator doors opening came from the other side of the store.

"The service elevators!" Mackenzie whispered. "He must be over there. Let's go!"

Quietly we headed over toward where Mackenzie

thought the service elevators were, but in the darkness, and with the way department stores lay out their counters and displays—so that you can never walk more than thirty feet in a straight line—we were soon totally disoriented.

"I think the elevators are that way," said Mackenzie, pointing to her left.

"I thought they were over there," I said, pointing to my right.

We sat tight for a moment, again listening intently. We heard someone moving in the distance behind us.

"Isn't that where we just came from?" Mackenzie whispered.

"I don't know," I said. "I'm so mixed up, I don't know where we are or where we've been. Remember when we found that body in the window? Once they lock the doors upstairs, they release patrol dogs—Dobermans, that like to snack on burglar served rare."

"Oh, nice. We'll end up as dog kibble."

Suddenly a heavy cart, loaded with knives and meat cleavers, rolled toward us out of the darkness.

"Mac, watch out!" I yelled, shoving her out of the way. The cart clipped me on the hip and knocked me down, but luckily none of the blades caught me. I caught a brief glimpse of someone scurrying away from us down a darkened aisle.

"P.C., are you okay?" Mackenzie said, patting me all over, looking for blood or bones sticking out.

"I'm fine," I said, getting up. "But someone's either trying to scare us off or kill us."

"Well, he's succeeded in scaring us," said Mackenzie. "Let's get out of here before he kills us."

"I'm with you," I said. "Sometimes discretion is the better part of valor, as Shakespeare said."

"Actually, it was 'The better part of valor is discretion,'" she corrected me. "*Henry IV*, Part I. We read it last semester, remember?"

"Show-off," I grunted. "Anyway, let's get out of here before we get sliced, diced, and julienned."

"Right behind you," she said, and we made for the direction I thought the escalators were in.

We bumbled through the dark for a while. Suddenly something clattered on the shelf next to Mackenzie's head and fell to the floor. I bent down to take a look.

"Mac!" I shouted. "Someone's throwing knives at us!"

Schwing! One stuck into the cardboard box of the bread machine I was standing next to.

We broke into a headlong run, Mackenzie in the lead. It was all I could do to keep up with her as she led the way through the darkened maze of the department-store basement. At one point I crashed into a tower of canned gourmet lobster bisque. Cans flew everywhere in a tremendous explosion of sound.

"Do you have any idea of how to get out of here?" I yelled at Mackenzie up ahead of me.

"No!" she said. "But if we keep running, we'll find an exit sooner or later."

Just as she said that, sure enough, we came upon the fire stairs that led up to the ground floor.

"Thank goodness!" Mackenzie said. "We're home free."

"I think you spoke too soon," I said. "Listen!" A deep, braying, barking sound echoed from the top of the stairwell. "Doberman! And it sounds like it's coming this way!"

Without thinking, we both took off as fast as we could away from the stairwell.

Running half-blind through the darkened space, we managed to make our way out of the appliances section of the floor and into the gourmet foods. I was leading the way this time, until suddenly I tripped over something and went sprawling.

Mackenzie screamed. The dog, still halfway across the store, barked like a hound of hell.

"I'm okay, Mac!" I said. "I'm okay!"

She screamed again.

"What's the matter?" I asked. "Why are you screaming?"

Mackenzie pointed down, and I saw what I had tripped over.

Paul Zachary lay face up, eyes horribly open but gone lifeless, on the cold linoleum floor. A funnel was jammed into his mouth.

8

Measuring

Now it was my turn to scream.

"P.C.!" said Mackenzie, regaining her senses. "Let's get out of here. That dog is going to be on top of us any second now!"

"Too late," I said, as the Hound of the Baskervilles came skittering around a corner, his toenails clicking on the hard floor. "Come on!" I grabbed Mackenzie's hand and pulled her behind the counter we'd been standing in front of. In the counter's cold case were piles of sausages, chops, and other meats. "Start throwing!"

Mackenzie picked up a bratwurst and fired it at the snarling brute. He leaped and snatched it out of the air in his fangs.

Chewing energetically, the dog gulped down the German delicacy in three chomps. He turned to us and barked again, but this one was a friendlier, more expectant sort of bark. His tail wagged.

"Catch, Fido!" I said, winging a sirloin at him like a Frisbee.

Again the dog caught it in the air and immediately set to chowing down.

"I don't know how long we can keep this up," I said. "What'll we do when he's not hungry anymore?"

"I don't know," said Mackenzie, heaving a leg of lamb. "Just keep throwing!"

Just then a shrill buzzing sounded, and all the lights came back on. The burglar alarm had been activated. The cops would be here any minute. Fido chewed away happily.

We were saved.

Two hours later Mackenzie and I were sitting with Lieutenant Cooper in his office at the Thirty-eighth Precinct. He'd called out for some Middle Eastern takeout, and we were scarfing down hummus, falafel, and tahini—regular, plain old normal New York street food, which I for one found a refreshing change after a day's talk of fish eggs and goose livers.

In between bites we gave Lieutenant Cooper the blow-by-blow on what had happened in North-Astor's basement.

"Foolish of you kids to be caught in the store after closing time," Lieutenant Cooper couldn't help pointing out, as if we weren't already aware of it. "You're lucky that Doberman didn't tear you to pieces."

"We're really sorry, Lieutenant Cooper," said Mackenzie. "We didn't do it on purpose, exactly."

"You're also lucky whoever killed Paul Zachary didn't get you, too," he reminded us.

"He tried," I said. "A couple of those knives nearly got us. At the time we thought it was Zachary himself who was trying to kill us. But there was someone else down there, sneaking around in the shadows."

"Gives me the willies just thinking about it," said Mackenzie, shivering.

"Whoever the murderer is, he or she is completely deranged," I said. "First the attempt on Julius that misfired and killed Billy Rose. And now the murder of Paul Zachary."

Lieutenant Cooper said, "At least now we have the perp on film."

I dropped my falafel and said, "Of course! Security cameras! Let's take a look."

Lieutenant Cooper escorted us from his office through a maze of hallways, to a room marked MEDIA CENTER. Inside was a confused jumble of TVs, reel-to-reels, VCRs, DVD and Laserdisk players, old-fashioned movie projectors, tape players, and CD boom boxes—whatever the cops might need to view whatever kind of evidence they might have.

A young officer, wearing a clip on his pocket that read LOGAN, was fast-forwarding through a grainy black-and-white videotape. It showed a blurry, unchanging view of a well-stocked shelf.

"Nothing on this one either," he said to Lieutenant

Cooper. "All but one of the tapes are like this one. Somebody smeared petroleum jelly on the lens of the camera. The video's too blurry to be used as evidence."

"There were seven cameras total in the basement, right?" Lieutenant Cooper said.

Officer Logan held up a videotape. "We got one good one," he said. "Caught the murderer in the act. Take a look."

On the screen we could see a grainy view of the meat department, where Zachary's body had been found. A little clock in the lower right-hand corner of the screen read 5:00.

"This tape covers the period from five o'clock until the moment when officers removed it from the camera," Logan explained. "The murder took place shortly after the store closed at seven."

He fast-forwarded through the tape. Clerks zipped around behind the counters. Customers rushed up, bobbing and weaving in that comical way people do when film is sped up. The store had been very busy at the beginning of the tape, but as seven o'clock closing time approached, fewer customers could be seen. Finally, a few minutes before seven, the last clerk left the area. Fifteen minutes after that, the lights went off.

"It's so dark, it's hard to see anything," I said.

"Just watch," Logan said. "You'll be surprised by what you can make out."

We were no longer fast-forwarding through the tape

now, but watching it in real time. After a few minutes, a man entered the frame.

"There's Zachary," Mackenzie said.

"It's surreal, watching a man in his last few moments on earth," I said, as on the screen, Zachary swiveled his head from side to side, and backed up toward the meat counter.

"He looks jumpy."

"Well, by this time the Doberman was barking and you'd knocked down a tower of cans," Mackenzie pointed out. "He must have thought all hell was breaking loose. No wonder he looks scared."

A second figure, creeping along behind the counter of the meat department, entered the frame. I got heebie-jeebie chills up my spine. Logan pressed a button to slow the tape down, and we now saw the action unfold at half speed.

Paul Zachary had his back up against the counter. I could imagine he was thinking the exact same thing Mackenzie and I had been thinking at that moment: How the heck am I going to get away from that dog?

Behind the counter, the second man, whose face was oddly pale—it seemed almost to shine in the darkness—ducked down and emerged holding an enormous Virginia ham, the kind that is basically the entire leg of a hog. Sneaking up behind Zachary, he slowly raised it above his head. He moved in a herky-jerky way, as if in some kind of trance. He lurched across the counter.

Zachary must have heard him move, because he started to spin around. But the murderer was ready for him. He brought the ham down in one swift, vicious motion and slammed Zachary on the head with it.

Zachary hit the floor as if he'd been shot in the heart. The hat went skittering out of the frame of the video-tape. The murderer raced around the counter with the ham and slammed it down again. Dropping the ham next to the body, he reached into the pocket of his coat and drew out a funnel, which he inserted into his victim's mouth.

"What's with the funnel?" I asked.

"Deranged killers often humiliate their victims in inexplicable ways," said Lieutenant Cooper.

The killer walked toward the camera and passed out of view.

"That's it," said Officer Logan, clicking off the tape. "The next thing that happens is you kids come into the picture, trip over the body, then start throwing meat at the dog. The lights come on, security shows up, and here we are."

"I'd like to see the face of the murderer again," said Lieutenant Cooper.

"Sure," said Officer Logan. "In fact, I can enhance it for you."

He rewound the tape, to the point where the murderer started walking toward the camera. He froze the picture.

"You can hardly see him," I said, squinting at the picture on the TV.

"Watch what this baby can do," said Officer Logan. "This is no ordinary VCR."

Pressing a couple of buttons on a remote, he caused the picture to brighten significantly. Then he enhanced the focus, and even zoomed in on the face of the murderer. We could now see it surprisingly clearly. But we still couldn't make out who it was.

"Look at that face," I said. "It doesn't even look human."

"It's horrible," said Mackenzie. "Like the face of a cadaver, or a zombie."

"Or someone wearing a mask," I said. "That's not the face of the murderer, it's a mask. . . . Looks like it's made out of dough. What a brilliant idea—you can wear it to kill someone, then go home and eat the evidence!"

"I think you're on to something, P.C.," said Lieutenant Cooper.

"Do you have any video coverage of the opening ceremonies where Billy Rose was killed?" I asked.

"We do," Lieutenant Cooper said. "Several films shot by official crews of the festival."

"Can we see them?" Mackenzie asked.

"Sure," said Lieutenant Cooper. "But not tonight. It's late, and you kids need to be getting home."

He was right about that. Earlier, I'd called my aunt Doris to let her know I was at the stationhouse with

Mackenzie. She'd gone ballistic. Apparently news of the two murders was all over the TV, and she knew me well enough to know I was probably in the middle of it. Plus, my dad was out of town—he'd taken off for Siberia the week before, to help dig a mastodon out of some permafrost—so Aunt Doris was responsible for me. I made it a point never to cross Aunt Doris.

Mackenzie had also called her parents. They already knew what she'd been up to. Dave Wisner, the assistant coroner, had reported to Mackenzie's mom that he'd run into her on the scene. So they were a little less freaked out than Aunt Doris had been, but still, they weren't too happy to learn their daughter had almost been devoured by a Doberman.

"Come back in the morning," Lieutenant Cooper said, "and I'll let you see those tapes."

"Deal," I said.

"Logan, will you give these kids a ride home in your squad car?"

During the ride to the Upper West Side, where both Mackenzie and I live, we took another look at *Come Fry with Me*, Robbie McGrath's book.

I paged through it until I got to the table of contents: a chill went up my spine as I read the names of Billy Rose and Paul Zachary. Billy Rose had been featured in the first section of the book, "Voices from the Future," which included an interview with Billy, as well as one of his favorite recipes: a wilted salad with honey-balsamic vinaigrette and roasted corn. The next section focused on Paul Zachary and included his signature recipe, the squab stuffed with foie gras.

"Mac, I think I understand the significance of the funnel," I said.

"Me too," she said. "Foie gras."

"Exactly. Zachary was famous for raising geese force-fed with funnels. The killer was playing a sick little joke on him by shoving a funnel into his mouth."

"Maybe it's coincidence, but this cookbook is like a recipe collection for murder," said Mackenzie. "Billy dies by salad; Zachary, like one of his geese."

"It's possible Julius wasn't the intended first victim after all," I said. "We'll have to rethink everyone's motive—Robbie's, for instance. We know why he'd want to kill Julius, but why kill Zachary? Seems like we know even less now than we did before."

"Maybe not," said Mackenzie. "I think we know who the next target is going to be." She pointed at the book, at the third name in the contents page.

"Vladimira Koncharovna," I read aloud.

"The Russian Wolfhound herself," said Mackenzie.

9

The Thrill of the Grill

The next morning Mackenzie and I met up again at Julio's Bagel Pagoda, the Cuban-Jewish-Chinese place on the corner of Seventieth and Broadway. Julio's has the best blintzes and espresso, plus first-rate dim sum.

Mackenzie came in wearing a typical Mackenzie outfit—little gold clothespin earrings, a sort of see-through lacy thing over a black T, pink leather miniskirt, and leopard-print Doc Martens.

"Care for an egg roll?" I asked. "Or a bagel with schmear?"

"Neither, thanks," she said. "I just finished off a box of Pop-Tarts at home."

"So what's the agenda for today?" I slurped at a miniature cup of thick coffee.

"There's an exhibition of ice sculptures at one. All the top restaurants will be contributing a statue for the show—the kind of thing they put together for a special event."

"Ice sculpture, eh? Sounds cool."

Mackenzie rolled her eyes at my lame joke. "You

know, I've been thinking," she said. "So far your aunt's connection with Julius LaCroix hasn't really gotten us anywhere with him, besides backstage at the opening ceremonies, of course. You know what would really convince him to cater our birthday party?"

"No, what?" I asked.

"If we saved his life! I mean, how could he refuse? He'd owe us big-time. He'd probably even do it for free. The kids at Westside High would just die!"

"Mac, there's a bloodthirsty side coming out in you over this whole birthday-party thing," I said.

"Everyone at Westside will be so jealous!"

"Calm down, Dr. Demento," I said. "First we have to save Julius. And how do you propose we do that?"

"Well . . . I hadn't totally figured that one out yet, actually."

I jumped as my cell phone vibrated in my back pocket. For a split second I flashed to the scorpion that had given me nightmares yesterday. Then I calmed down, took my phone out of my pocket, and answered it. "Hello?"

"P.C., it's me, Jesus."

"Jesus, buddy, what's up?"

"Hey, nothing much. I've been seeing on the news this zombie killer guy at the foodfest. Man, you and Mac should stay out of this one. That guy's a freak. It's too dangerous."

"Never fear, Jesus," I said. "We've got it all under

control." I winked at Mackenzie. She knew as well as I did that we didn't have a darn thing under control.

"Do you have anything for us?" I asked him before he could try to talk me out of anything.

"Not much. GothamGourmet.com says Billy Rose was from Lafayette, Louisiana, the same town Julius LaCroix was from. Modeled his career on Julius's. And speaking of Julius, according to *The Wall Street Journal*, his restaurant is in financial trouble. It's been hemorrhaging moolah like there's no tomorrow. Julius has an investment partner with a controlling interest in L'Aventure, and there are rumors that the partner's planning on shutting him down."

I whistled. "Sounds bad. We had no idea Julius was in such trouble. Maybe we can get him to do the party even if we don't save his life."

"What?" Jesus said.

"Never mind. Hey, can you find out for me where in New York I might be able to get a scorpion—you know, as a pet?"

"P.C., you are one weird dude."

"It's not for me," I said. "Honestly."

"Sure, sure. You have a 'friend' who needs a scorpion. Right. I'll get right on it."

"Thanks, buddy. Catch you later."

Mackenzie laughed. "So now Jesus thinks you want a scorpion for a pet?"

"My apartment building doesn't allow dogs," I said. I filled her in on what Jesus had told me about Julius's financial troubles. "So where to, Mac?"

"I'd say it's time we drop by L'Aventure—to talk to Julius, and to grill Robbie."

"Agreed."

Half an hour later we were in the back offices of L'Aventure, on East Eighty-first Street, a block from the Metropolitan Museum of Art, in what's probably the swankiest neighborhood in the whole world. We hadn't had too much trouble talking our way past Jean-Claude, the maitre d'. People tend to give way when you start bandying about phrases like "murder investigation" and "your boss's life may be in danger."

Julius sat slumped behind a disorderly desk. He looked older even than his sixty years—gaunt, with huge bags under his eyes, as if he hadn't been sleeping well. And who could blame him, considering he might be the target of a maniac?

Robbie McGrath bustled around the office. Unlike yesterday, he seemed nervous, shuffling papers, exclaiming over a misplaced invoice, and generally adding to the stress level.

"I simply have no idea why anyone would want to kill Billy Rose or Paul Zachary," he said, in response to our questions. "Of course, Zachary had enemies—he'd played dirty pool with too many people over the years not to have earned some hatred. But . . . murder? It's unthinkable!"

"Obviously, *someone* thought of it," I said.

There was a soft tap at the door, and Jean-Claude stuck his head in. "Mr. McGrath?"

"What is it, Jean-Claude?" Robbie snapped.

"The champagne flutes are coming out of the dishwasher spotted again, and Raymond refuses to—"

"Okay, okay, I'm coming," Robbie sighed. "I have to handle everything around here! You'll be all right, Julius?"

"I'll be fine, Robbie," Julius said.

Robbie left us in the office alone with Julius, who was massaging his chest.

"You seem tired, Mr. LaCroix," Mackenzie said. "Are you feeling okay?"

"This whole situation has exacerbated my angina," he said. "I've had two small heart attacks, and the doctors have told me I should avoid stress. If I live through the week, it'll be a miracle."

"I'm very sorry to hear that," I said. "This must be a very difficult time for you."

"Why would anyone want to kill me? I'm not going to live much longer anyway. Last year I had a quadruple bypass. I've got terrible arthritis." He held up his hands, as if we could tell just by looking at them what kind of pain he was in.

"I noticed you often walk with a limp," Mackenzie said. "Is that the arthritis too?"

"No, dear me, no. For years I've suffered from plantar fascitis in my left foot."

"Plantar fascitis," I said. "That's like bone spurs, right?"

"Similar, my boy. Very painful. And yet I do my best."

"And your fans appreciate it, Mr. LaCroix," Mackenzie said, buttering him up like a croissant.

"Well, I've always put a hundred percent into this business, treated other chefs with the utmost generosity. And now I'm just a sad, broken-down old man. . . ."

There was no doubt Julius was trying to win our sympathies by playing the pathetic victim. He was all raindrops and weeping strings, but for some reason, I had my doubts about the sincerity of the act.

"I feel so guilty about Billy Rose's death," Julius went on. "A poisoned salad meant for me. Oh, why didn't I eat it? Why? It should have been me, a useless old man whose life is behind him, instead of poor Billy, so young, so full of promise."

Robbie came bustling back into the office. "Julius, you really shouldn't upset yourself so!" Turning to us, he said, "Mr. LaCroix needs to rest now. We have a show to do this afternoon, and we don't want to let the people down."

"Yes, I do feel tired. Perhaps we can continue this another time?"

Robbie helped Julius to his feet and through a door in the back of the office. There was a cot in the little room in back. "Why don't you take a short nap, Julius," he said, closing the door on the old chef.

"Will he be all right, Mr. McGrath?" asked Mac.

"Chef LaCroix feels such an obligation to the public," Robbie said to us. "The joy he brings his fans is really what keeps him going. But sometimes he overdoes it. He's ruining his health."

"Mr. McGrath, who do you think killed Billy Rose and Paul Zachary?" I asked, getting straight to the point.

"Why, I couldn't say," said Robbie. "I honestly have no idea."

"Were you aware that the murders seem to be taking place in the same order as the recipes in the book you compiled?"

"What?" he said. "What a terrible coincidence!"

"What's more," I continued, "Billy Rose was killed by a salad, just like the one in the book. And Paul Zachary was found with a funnel in his mouth like a fattened goose. Still a coincidence?"

"I don't know what you're driving at," said Robbie, suddenly seeming defensive, "but if you're insinuating that I had anything to do with—"

Jean-Claude put his head in the office again. "I'm

sorry to bother you, Mr. McGrath, but I believe some-one's been watering down the Glenfiddich again. Henri denies it, but I'm quite certain that—"

"Okay, okay, I'm coming," said Robbie. He stood to go. "I really must go now."

"We understand," I said.

"We'll let ourselves out," Mackenzie added as Robbie left the office.

As soon as he shut the door, we sprang into action. "Okay," I whispered. "We only have a few min-utes before he'll get suspicious—or before he'll be back to check on Julius."

I scooted to a file cabinet, and Mackenzie ran behind the desk and started opening drawers.

I found a file marked PERSONAL/LEGAL, yanked it out of the cabinet, and set it on the desk. Inside were a bunch of financial papers—car insurance records, investment account statements, that sort of thing.

"Bingo," I murmured, pulling out a stapled-together bundle of papers entitled "Last Will and Testament of Julius Leo LaCroix."

"What've you got, P.C.?" Mackenzie asked.

"Julius's will," I said. "It says here that one Robert James McGrath is the sole heir and beneficiary of Julius's estate, yadda yadda . . . Oh, wait—it also says that Robbie is his son—and that he's sorry for never acknowledging him."

"But Deborah Hudson said that Julius never had any children."

"I guess it was a deep, dark secret—and maybe a motive for murder?" I said.

"You may be right, P.C.," said Mackenzie. "Look what I found. Robbie's credit-card statement, with charges from Bally's Atlantic City, Caesar's Palace, the Trump Castle Casino." She flipped through the receipts. "Also Belmont Racetrack and Freehold Raceway. And there are hundreds of charges from something called Gamblingheaven.com."

"Sounds like Robbie has a bit of a gambling problem," I said.

"So there's your motive," said Mackenzie. "If Robbie needed cash to feed the monkey, he'd know where to get it—but Julius would have to kick the bucket first."

"And Robbie probably resented him for not acknowledging him as his son."

Suddenly we heard someone's footsteps in the hallway outside the office. Scrambling fast, we stuffed the various papers back into the appropriate drawers and files, just as Robbie came back in.

"We were just leaving," I said casually as we walked out the door.

He gave us a suspicious look. "I should say so."

Back out on the street, Mackenzie blew a big sigh of relief. "Whew! That was close. He'd have been pretty peeved if he'd caught us going through his files. So whaddaya think, P.C.?"

"It's the same old story," I said. "Where there's a will, there's a beneficiary. And if Robbie *is* the murderer, it's even worse—it's patricide."

10

Revenge Is a Dish Best Served Cold

"Maybe it's true that Robbie wants to murder Julius to inherit his money," said Mackenzie. "That would explain how Billy got killed accidentally. But it wouldn't explain why he'd kill Paul Zachary."

"Unless he murdered Zachary to throw us off the scent," I said. "The zombie killer we saw on that tape looked crazy enough to do it. And who knows? He might've developed a taste for murder."

"Vladimira Koncharovna's recipe was next in Robbie's cookbook."

"We should get back to the festival right away," I said. "Someone should warn old Vladi that she may be next in line for an icing."

We took a cab, which whizzed us down Park Avenue as far as Fiftieth Street, before we got bogged down in the crowds overflowing from the festival. "The publicity surrounding the murders doesn't seem to have hurt the festival," Mackenzie said.

"Never underestimate the drawing power of violent crime," I said, paying the cabbie.

We walked to the *Gourmet Zone* set, where Julius would be shooting his show later in the day. We spotted Lieutenant Cooper, directing some uniformed cops who were setting up crowd-control barriers along the sidewalk, and clued him in on our working theory.

"Doesn't seem likely," said Lieutenant Cooper. "Though it's mighty odd that the two victims were the authors of the first two recipes."

"And the way they were killed was straight out of the book," I pointed out.

"I'll have my men run regular checks on Vladimira Koncharovna and Danny Moran," Lieutenant Cooper said. He gave the stress ball he always carried a squeeze.

"As safe as they can be at a festival with a couple hundred thousand people milling about," Mackenzie said.

"Lieutenant Cooper, Mac and I were wondering if we could take another look at the videotape of the killer," I said.

"I was just on my way to our temporary station across the street," said Lieutenant Cooper. "We wanted to keep an eye on things from close by. Come on."

The temporary headquarters was located on the second floor of an office building across Fifth Avenue from St. Patrick's Cathedral. Large picture windows gave us a perfect view of the *Gourmet Zone* set.

Lieutenant Cooper had Officer Logan, who was back on duty also, cue up the videotape of Paul Zachary's murder and went to take a phone call.

"Do you mind if I use that?" I asked him, pointing to the remote control.

"Sure," said Officer Logan. "Just don't erase anything."

I fast-forwarded to the point where the killer started walking toward the camera.

"Hmmm . . . he's pretty tall. It could have been Robbie, don't you think, Mac?"

"I don't know. Robbie's kind of skinny. You'd have to be really strong to bash someone's head in with a ham."

"You're probably right. Gotcha," I murmured, freezing the image. I zoomed in on the wrinkly, pasty-white visage.

"Really does look like a zombie," I said to Mackenzie. "There's something about that face that's bugging me, like there's a clue here somewhere but I can't put my finger on it."

"You don't think you can recognize someone beneath that mask, do you, P.C.?" Mackenzie asked. "Because I sure can't."

"No, that's not it exactly. It's just there's something on the tip of my brain, but . . ." I rewound the tape a little, then watched the murder again, this time in slo-mo.

"I did a report on zombies back in seventh grade," I said, gazing at the gruesome images on the TV screen. "There are conjure-men in Haiti who have the power to steal a man's soul, then reanimate the corpse. Emptied of the soul, the carcass can be sold for food."

"Oh, barf," said Mackenzie.

"The zombie monster can be killed by stabbing it in the heart, like a Balkan vampire," I went on. "Or by feeding it salt."

"Very culinary," Mackenzie said.

"Only a chef would think of wearing a mask of dough. I called your dad at his office this morning, Mac, and asked him what he thought. Mr. Riggs is a psychologist," I explained to Officer Logan.

"What did he say?" she asked.

"I asked him if he'd ever heard of a murderer who wore dough. He said the killer definitely picked such a weird modus operandi for a reason—at least a subconscious reason."

"You might want to take a look at these, too," said Officer Logan, handing me three more videotapes.

"I thought you said the other security cameras had been smeared with petroleum jelly," I said.

"I did," said Officer Logan. "Though it turns out it was butter."

"We should have guessed," said Mackenzie. "A killer chef would use butter."

"These tapes aren't from the department store," said Officer Logan. "These are tapes of the first murder shot by official camera crews of the festival."

"Maybe they show something we missed in person," Mackenzie said.

Officer Logan popped the first one in the VCR. It was

of surprisingly crummy quality, considering it was supposedly shot by a pro. It was taken from the edge of the stage, and showed the chefs arriving one by one, Deborah Hudson greeting them, the chefs saying hello to one another, and so on. The sound of the mob, and the music blaring from the loudspeakers, drowned out everything being said.

Each of the chefs came near to one of the tubs of oleander at one time or another, but nowhere did the tapes capture anyone actually plucking off any of the plant.

"There's opportunity galore," I said, "but no hard evidence implicating anybody."

The other two tapes showed more of the same. There was Billy with Julius, just moments before his death. In the third tape, shot by the photographer closest to center stage, you could almost hear what Billy and Julius were talking about, but crowd noises drowned the conversation out.

"We've gone over the tapes a hundred times," said Lieutenant Cooper. "There's nothing conclusive there. All the chefs, plus Deborah Hudson, came near the oleander at various points. It could have been any one of them that poisoned Billy Rose. Heck, for that matter it could have been suicide."

"Paul Zachary wasn't a suicide, though," I said. "Speaking of which, have you asked the chefs where they were yesterday at seven P.M., when Zachary was getting bludgeoned with a ham?"

"Danny Moran and Deborah Hudson are each other's alibi—they claim to have been together at the time of Zachary's death," said Lieutenant Cooper.

"That much is believable," Mackenzie said.

"Ms. Koncharovna has no alibi. She said she was in her restaurant, alone, when the murder occurred."

"Huh," I said. "What about Julius?"

"He was seeing his doctor. His heart specialist is Dr. Halperin from Mt. Sinai. Luckily, he was at the festival—he examined Julius backstage to make certain everything was okay after the scorpion bite. After that, Robbie said he dropped Julius off at one of his other cardiologists, at 40 Central Park South, right next to the Plaza. Dr. Pizzano."

"Did the alibi check out?" I asked.

"Dr. Pizzano confirmed that Julius had been in to see him."

"We're getting close to cracking this case," I said. "I can feel it. But in the meantime, we've got to go talk to Vladimira. I'd be interested in hearing her take on the murders."

"And besides, we need to warn her," added Mackenzie.

"Warn her?" asked the lieutenant.

"That she might be next."

Into the Fire

We could hear the Russian music blaring from three blocks away. The street in front of I, Caviar appeared at first to be a scene of utter confusion—the crowd stood twenty deep, and up on a raised platform Vladimira presided over a gigantic grill.

Jugglers tossed swords twenty feet in the air, tumblers somersaulted over each other, mustachioed men did that weird Russian chorus-line Chuck Berry dance where you cross your arms, squat down on your heels, and kick your feet out.

Flames shot up six feet over Vladimira's head as she placed swords loaded with huge chunks of sturgeon, tomatoes, and onions on the red-hot grill. When the fish and vegetables were done, Vladimira pulled each sword from the grill with a flourish.

"Looks delicious!" Mackenzie exclaimed.

Dancing girls in skimpy outfits that exposed beaucoup de navel raced up, bearing huge trays loaded with saffron rice and grilled figs.

"You ain't kidding," I said.

Deftly Vladimira slid the steaming delicacies off a sword, then turned to the grill for the next load. The dancing girl plunged into the hungry masses waiting to be fed. What appeared at first to be confusion was in fact a carefully choreographed performance. Vladimira and her staff operated in controlled chaos, like a well-oiled machine.

Mackenzie and I managed to worm our way through the crowd up to the front door of the restaurant, which was basically empty. Since they were giving away food on the street, why would anyone be inside paying for it?

"Whew!" I said, wiping my brow. "I feel worn out just watching old Vladi. She's some performer!"

"For sure," Mackenzie said.

"That shish kebab looked pretty tasty."

"Shashlik," Mackenzie corrected me. "Russians call it shashlik."

"Whatever."

Just then Vladimira came bursting through the front doors of the restaurant. She looked exhausted. Her floor-length black evening gown was drenched with sweat, and her face was flushed from the heat of the grill and from slinging all those heavy swords around.

Her unibrowed bodyguard followed her. I raised my eyebrows at Mackenzie. Now *he* looked strong enough to bludgeon someone with a ham.

Mackenzie grabbed a glass of ice water off a nearby table and handed it to Vladimira, who swigged it down as if she'd just spent thirty days lost in the Sahara.

"Another triumph!" she said, slamming the glass down on the maitre d's podium. "There's not a person out there who'll forget today's show. My staff performed impeccably, the shashlik was exquisite, and I was my usual brilliant self." As if noticing us for the first time, she said, "And who are you? Wait! Don't tell me! You two were there when Mr. Rose was poisoned."

"That's right," said Mackenzie.

"I never forget a face!" Vladimira crowed. She was still full of adrenaline from the show.

"We're investigating the murders of Billy Rose and Paul Zachary," I explained. "We need to talk to you. Is there somewhere we can go to speak in private?"

"Follow me!" she commanded, in a voice she must have learned in Red Army boot camp. "Gunther, you stay—I'm sure I have nothing to fear from these two children."

Gunther stayed put. I wondered if he ever spoke.

Vladimira led us through a wonderland of red velvet and gold leaf—"understated" was not a term that could ever be applied to I, Caviar—to a small office at the back of the restaurant. We sat down, and Mackenzie said, "We're afraid you're in danger, Ms. Koncharovna."

We explained our theory that the killer was using Robbie McGrath's cookbook as a blueprint for murder. "And yours is the next recipe in the book," I concluded.

"Nonsense!" Vladimira said, though I could tell she was taking us very seriously indeed. The flush had gone out of her face. "No one would dare try to kill me. I have Gunther." She reached into the drawer of the desk she was sitting behind. "And if someone was foolish enough to try, I also have this!" she said, holding up a small, pearl-handled revolver. "And believe me, I know how to shoot. My father was a colonel in the Red Army."

That would explain the drill sergeant's voice, I thought to myself. Aloud, I asked, "If you're sure no one would try to kill you, why keep a gun?"

"Better safe than sorry, as you Americans say." She put the gun on the desktop and patted it fondly. "In Russia, we say 'Kill the fox first, eat the chickens later.'"

Mackenzie and I looked at her blankly.

"Perhaps it loses something in translation," she said.

"I'm glad you feel protected, Ms. Koncharovna," Mackenzie started up again. "Now, maybe you can tell us a little about your relationship with Paul Zachary. I got the feeling you and he weren't too fond of each other."

"No," she said. "Paul Zachary and I didn't mix. We were rivals, not friends. Still, I regret his unfortunate death. He will be missed."

Just not by you, I added silently.

"As for Julius LaCroix," she continued, "he would not be missed by anybody. Anybody! Well, perhaps the weasel Robbie McGrath will shed a tear when the great man goes. But no one else! Julius LaCroix has shafted, as you say, too many people in this business. He has enemies everywhere."

"Like you, Ms. Koncharovna?" I asked. For a second, I thought she was going to rip my throat out. Mackenzie dug her fingernails into my hand as Vladimira picked up her revolver and slowly raised it in our direction. Then she stood up, picked up her handbag, and put the revolver in it. I exhaled.

"Now, if you will excuse me," she said, "I have to go to Radio City. They're storing our ice sculpture for this afternoon's show. I, Caviar's is a magnificent Siberian tiger."

Vladimira force-marched us back through the restaurant and out the doors. The crowd was still milling around, finishing their plates of shashlik. The jugglers and dancers leaped around to the blare of the "Russian Dance" from the *Nutcracker Suite* on the loudspeaker.

"Roll over, Beethoven," I muttered, as Mackenzie and I fought our way through the crowd. "And tell Tchaikovsky the news."

"What news is that, P.C.?"

"The news is, old Vladi's more freaked out by Zachary's death than she's letting on," I said. "She was gripping that pistol like it was the only thing standing between her and certain death."

"I noticed that too. She's definitely hiding something."

"But what?" I asked. "That's the question. What is she not telling us?"

12

Sugar and Spice and Everything Nasty

"We've got enough suspects to fill up the prime-time schedule on the Food Network," I said as we made our way back downtown. I ticked them off on my fingers. "There's Julius LaCroix. Robbie McGrath. Vladimira Koncharovna. Gunther. They're all tall enough to be the zombie killer."

"At least we don't have to suspect Paul Zachary anymore," said Mackenzie. "Him being dead and all."

"Yes, that is convenient," I said. "Maybe the process of elimination—permanent elimination—will solve this case for us. Last one standing is the murderer."

"We can only hope," said Mackenzie.

It was grim humor, but we were feeling pretty grim.

"Look, there's Danny Moran," said Mackenzie.

We were just going through the revolving-door entrance to the Turf Club, hoping to find Danny, as he was going out.

I tapped on the glass to get his attention. Mackenzie and I did a full 360 through the door and landed back out on the sidewalk again.

"Mr. Moran—" I started.

"No autographs now, kid," Danny said. "Come by the place later, maybe we could use another busboy." He looked Mackenzie up and down. "Ever think about hostessing, toots?"

"I'm more the karate-instructor type," Mackenzie said. "But thanks, anyway. We're not here to get your autograph or apply for jobs."

"Whaddaya want, then?" Danny said, bounding up the sidewalk.

We explained who we were, and Danny said, "Oh yeah, now I recognize you."

He walked with a quick, powerful little swagger, like a boxer answering the bell. "I'm on my way to the ice rink, to make sure the sculpture is ready for tonight's show. It's a statue of those two kids who got suckled by a wolf and founded Rome."

"Romulus and Remus," I said.

"Yeah, those're the guys. I wanted food and action. It's a beaut—you oughta see it."

"Sounds nice," said Mackenzie. "We'd like to ask you some questions, though. Do you have a minute?"

"I always got a minute for pretty girl," he said. "Just not right now. Come in to the restaurant after hours some time, we'll fix you up. Lose the army boots, babe, and you could be one sweet little hostess."

Mackenzie ignored his super-sexist remarks and asked, "Who do you think would want to kill Julius LaCroix?"

"Hey, what do I look like, Sherlock Holmes? How should I know who'd want to whack the old coot? Practically anybody who's ever met him, except maybe a sales rep from the Tums company. I gotta go. Catch you later, toots."

He took off at dead run up the avenue. We realized it was pointless to try to keep up with him. He wasn't interested in talking to us, at least about the murders.

"What a jerk," said Mackenzie.

"Yeah, he's got a lot of nerve," I said. "He didn't call *me* 'toots' even once."

Mackenzie slapped me on the shoulder. "Take that, toots," she said. "Happy now?"

Rubbing my arm, I replied, "It'll do. So who do we go see now? Deborah? I'd bet the Ice Princess would knock off anyone to see lover boy move up the food chain."

Mackenzie looked at me thoughtfully. "Maybe so. But I don't get a coldhearted-killer vibe from her, or from Danny, either. He may be obnoxious, but I don't think he's a murderer."

"A lover, not a fighter, huh?"

"Something like that," said Mackenzie. "I think we should pay a visit to Julius's doctor. Whaddaya think, babe?"

"Right behind you, toots."

We headed uptown, toward the Park. Mackenzie checked the memo pad she'd been taking notes on, and found the address. Forty Central Park South. Dr. Pizzano, out of Mt. Sinai Hospital.

A little while later we were in the lobby of the office building where Dr. Pizzano had his office.

Without looking up from the *Maxim* magazine he was engrossed in, the concierge behind the reception desk asked, "May I help you?"

"We're here to see Dr. Pizzano," I said. "The cardiologist."

The concierge looked up, took off his reading glasses, and peered at us quizzically. "You must be looking for a different Dr. Pizzano."

"I'm sorry," I said, confused. "What do you mean?"

"We have a Dr. Pizzano in suite 1401," said the concierge. "But he's no cardiologist. He's a podiatrist—a foot doctor. But he's not in now. Doesn't have office hours on Sunday."

"I don't understand," I said. "The cops told us—"

"I know what happened," Mackenzie interrupted, snapping her fingers. "Julius told the cops he'd gone to the doctor, and gave them Dr. Pizzano's name. Lieutenant Cooper must have assumed that since he had a heart problem, Dr. Pizzano was another of his cardiologists. It was a simple mix-up."

"You're right," I said. I turned back to the concierge. "Did a very tall man—white haired, distinguished-looking, walks with a cane—come here for an appointment yesterday afternoon?"

"You must mean Chef LaCroix," said the concierge. "Oh, sure, he was here yesterday. He's one of Dr. Pizzano's best patients. One of my favorites too, always gives me a kitchen tip. Why, just yesterday he told me how I should use a turkey baster to squeeze pancake batter onto the griddle. I'm going to try it!"

"You do that," I said. "And don't forget to add a couple of drops of vanilla extract to the batter."

"I'll try that too."

Back out on the street, Mackenzie said, "I had no idea you knew how to make pancakes."

"I'm the pancake king," I said. "Waffles, too."

"Who'd-a thunk it?" said Mackenzie.

"So—Julius's doctor's appointment was with a podiatrist," I said. "I have a feeling it means something, but I can't figure out what. Let's call Jesus, see if he's dug up anything." I whipped out my cell phone and hit the speed dial.

"*Hola?*"

"Dude," I said. "It's me. Whatcha got?"

"Hey, P.C.," said Jesus. "I found out about scorpions. There are only two pet shops in the city that carry scorpions. They also carry tarantulas, if you're in the market for one."

"No thanks, I'll stick to goldfish," I said. "Where are these pet stores?"

"One's on Staten Island, so I don't think that's the one you want," said Jesus. "The other is called Tooth and

Claw. It's on West Forty-second Street, over near Tenth Avenue."

"Thanks, man," I said. "We'll check it out."

"One other thing," said Jesus. "I happened to notice something in an old newspaper article about Julius LaCroix that was posted on the Internet. Seems he and Paul Zachary were partners years ago in a bar on Fire Island called the Scorpion Room. Interesting, huh?"

"Very," I agreed.

"The article mentioned that the bar went bankrupt—there were accusations all around. A nasty blowup. That's when Julius and Paul had their falling out."

"See if you can find out who the money man is behind L'Aventure nowadays, all right?" I asked.

"Will do," said Jesus.

"Thanks, buddy. Talk to you later. *Ciao.*"

"*Adiós.*"

"Hail us a cab, Mac," I said. "We're going to West Forty-second Street."

13

Stewing

Tooth and Claw was a dark, crowded old store that smelled of wood shavings, wet fur, and stale water. Cages full of all sorts of bizarre creatures—snakes, iguanas, ferrets, skunks, big fat hairy spiders—lined the walls floor to ceiling. A plump, bald-headed guy with a lip ring sat behind the counter.

"Excuse me," I said, breaking into his comic-book reading. "Do you carry scorpions?"

Without looking up from the adventures of Spider Man, the clerk pointed to the far wall. Mackenzie and I picked our way past the bags of rat chow that cluttered the aisle. At the back of the store, underneath a bank of aquariums stocked with piranhas, baby sharks, and miniature barracudas, was a line of terrariums that held vicious-looking scorpions of the exact type that had stung Julius.

"Nasty-looking buggers, aren't they?" I said.

"Not quite as cuddly as a kitten, that's for sure," Mackenzie agreed.

We returned to the front of the store. Mackenzie asked, "Has anyone bought a scorpion recently?"

The clerk finally looked up. "We don't sell many of those pretty beasties. Guy came in here just yesterday, though. Wanted a lively one."

"Really," I said. "Do you remember what he looked like?"

"Do I remember?" The clerk shook his head. "How could I forget? He was all dolled up in sequins and cowboy hat. Rings on his fingers. Probably had bells on his toes, too. Looked like Liberace on Dress-to-Excess Day."

"You didn't happen to catch his name, did you?" I asked, though it was obvious who it must have been.

"Naw. Look, I wasn't really paying that much attention to the guy. We get weirdos in here all the time."

"Thanks for the info," I said.

He was deep into his reading again and didn't respond.

Out on the street, Mackenzie stepped to the curb to hail a taxi. Maybe it's just her ability to whistle through her fingers, but for some reason Mac can always get cab drivers' attention faster than I can. Sure enough, a taxi immediately screeched to a halt for her.

"Fiftieth and Fifth," Mackenzie told the driver. "Across from St. Patrick's."

We were headed back to Lieutenant Cooper's temporary HQ. We wanted to check out those videotapes again.

"This zombie thing really bothers me," I said as the

cab fought through the perpetual pandemonium that was Times Square. "It's as if there's something staring us straight in the face and we're not seeing it. I still think it's no accident our little maniac is wearing dough."

"As if someone wanted a last-minute disguise, but when they looked in their closet all they could find was flour, water, and yeast," said Mackenzie.

"Exactly," I said.

At the temporary HQ we asked to see Lieutenant Cooper. He wasn't in, but Officer Logan said we could run through the tapes again if we wanted.

"In fact, we have a new one," he said. "A German tourist happened to catch Billy Rose's death on tape. He shot the scene from the statue of General Sherman."

"He was up on the statue?" I asked.

"Perched on one of the hooves," Officer Logan said.

"I'd like to look at the fest's tapes again first," I said.

"We've transferred them in digital form to a computer, for closer analysis," said Officer Logan. "Let me show you."

He led us into a room similar to the one at the precinct that was stuffed full of equipment. Sitting down in front of a computer, he booted it and called up a program that played digitized videotape.

"Here's the first one," he said. He gave me and Mackenzie brief instructions on how to manipulate the images—slo-mo, zoom in, focus, that sort of thing. Then he left us to examine the tapes.

Going through the first two tapes, we weren't able to see anything we hadn't seen the first time. Watching the third tape, though, Mackenzie said, "Is that Billy's voice, underneath all the other racket?"

I jumped back through the tape and replayed the section. It showed Billy and Julius huddled together. Billy was chatting animatedly, recounting something he was obviously excited about. We could hear him say the words "Crumfeld," "St. John," and "Lafayette."

"I wonder if we can clean up the sound," I said, scanning the program's menu of effects. With a few minutes' work, by cutting the treble and bass, boosting the midrange, and cleaning up extraneous pops and rattles, we were able to hear what Billy Rose had been saying to Julius.

"Isn't it exciting!" [said Billy] "Ronald Crumfeld called me up out of the blue earlier this week and offered me the position of head chef at his new restaurant, Willow at the Edge of the Forest."

I paused the tape. "Didn't you tell me *Julius* was going to be head chef there?"

Mackenzie looked surprised. "He was supposed to be. All the gossip said he was Crumfeld's top choice. I guess Crumfeld changed his mind."

Looking at the paused image of Julius, a stricken expression on his lined face as Billy told him of his unexpected good fortune, told me all I needed to know about how the older chef had taken this news.

"He looks absolutely devastated," I said. "Crushed."

"Desperate," said Mackenzie. "Defeated."

We listened to the tape of Billy and Julius talking a little while longer, then moved to the VCR. We cued up the tape made by the German tourist on Sherman's horse. It showed the same events as the other three had—all the chefs, plus Deborah Hudson, near enough at one time or another to the pots of oleander to have had opportunity to pluck some leaves. We got to the point where Deborah Hudson handed the salad to Billy.

"Freeze!" Mackenzie said, and I paused the image.

"What?" I asked. "What do you see?"

"Look at the expression on Paul Zachary's face," said Mackenzie.

The other three tapes, all taken from angles lower down on the stage, had failed to capture Zachary's facial expression clearly at this particular moment. It was clear what it was, however.

"He's grimacing," I said. "He's watching Billy take the salad, and he's reacting with disgust *before* Billy even puts any in his mouth."

"He knew," Mackenzie whispered. "He knew the salad was poisoned."

"Which means either he was Billy's killer," I said, "or he saw someone else put the oleander in, and that someone killed him to keep him quiet."

"We're close to cracking the case, P.C."

"But a murder case is like a great stew," I said. "Every

ingredient has to be there, and this one's still missing something."

I checked my watch, then grabbed Mackenzie's hand.

"Let's go," I said.

"Where to?"

"I have a feeling we'll find the missing ingredient on ice."

Death à la Mode

"Vladimira said the ice sculptures for tonight's show were stored at Radio City," I said. "I'll bet you anything that's where we'll find Vladimira—and Danny Moran, too."

It wasn't a long walk crosstown to Radio City Music Hall, home of the famous Rockettes, but where we were hoping to find famous chefs. And just as we were approaching the Music Hall doors, we saw Robbie McGrath going in a stage door on the side of the building.

"After him, Watson," I said, racing to catch the door before it latched shut. I caught it just in time. Waiting a beat, giving Robbie time to get away from the door, I pulled the door open and we slipped inside. It took several seconds before our eyes adjusted to the darkened backstage hallway. We stood in the shadows, listening for the sound of Robbie's footsteps.

"I think he went that way," I whispered to Mackenzie, taking her hand and leading her inside. Unfortunately, we soon lost Robbie in the labyrinth of corridors.

Passageways branched off at crazy angles, seeming to double back on themselves and intersect unexpectedly. Dozens of unmarked doors, some locked, some unlocked, turned us around till we were completely disoriented.

"Where'd Robbie go?" I asked.

"I have no idea."

We wandered through the spooky backstage murk, going down stairs, climbing back up again, burrowing ever deeper into the twisted confusion beneath Radio City. Racks of costumes, glitter and rhinestones twinkling like burned-out stars, clogged the halls, and at times we had to literally climb over props.

"Cold air," Mackenzie said suddenly. "This way. The rink."

Following the frigid air billowing down one of the corridors, we finally came out into a huge room—the ice rink. Stored on the ice were the sculptures: a gigantic bear, mouth agape and huge paws raised in anger; a vicious hawk, its daggerlike talons spread; an enormous, glittering, translucent T. Rex like something out of a nightmare movie called *Ice Capades vs. Jurassic Park*. It seemed like every top-notch restaurant in New York had sponsored a sculpture. I spotted a gorilla, an anaconda wrestling a man, Danny's wolf. . . .

"So where's Robbie now?" I asked. "If he wasn't going into Radio City to check on his sculpture, what was he here for?"

"Robbie?" Mackenzie called. "Mr. McGrath?"

No answer.

"Anyone?" I yelled. My voice echoed into nothingness. No response.

"Let's get out of here, P.C.," Mackenzie said. "I have a bad feeling about this."

We were just turning to leave when I noticed, in the dim half-dark, wet drippings on the floor, as if footprints, leading from the rink.

"What's this?" I kneeled to take a closer look. In the dark, I couldn't tell what color the footprints were. "Smudged footprints—and smear marks, as if something was dragged across the floor."

We followed the footprints through a doorway and into a smaller room, where a row of plastic garment bags hung against the far wall. The smear marks disappeared under the bags. Mackenzie crossed the room and started going through the bags, moving them on their hangers as if she were shopping for a dress. They were on a chain-belt conveyor, like at the dry cleaners'.

I got a sinking feeling in the pit of my stomach as Mackenzie found the button to start up the conveyer. "I wouldn't do that if I were you, Mac. . . ." I said.

But she pressed the button anyway, and the bags began to move, marching like mindless phantoms. Suddenly Robbie burst out from behind the silently gliding specters. Mackenzie jumped back, startled. Robbie stood frozen, staring at her, a look of utter horror etched on his face. No one said anything for a long, totally bizarre moment. Mackenzie and I stared in complete shock at him, and he stared back at us. All at once he shoved past us and raced for the door.

Mackenzie started to make a move to go after him, but stopped when one especially grotesque plastic garment bag swung around the bend and into view.

"Mac!" I said, the full horror of what I was seeing begining to dawn on me. "Look!"

She spun around and hit the button, causing the conveyor belt to stop.

Pressed against the translucent plastic of one of the bags we could see a person's face, her mouth open, her eyes rolled back in their sockets.

"P.C.," Mackenzie said. "It's—"

"Vladimira," I finished for her.

Just then the body slipped out of the bag with a sickening *slurp* sound and hit the floor, blood splattering all around it. She lay in a distorted heap. Next to her was her handbag, flung open and empty. And through her neck was a long, swordlike skewer.

We dashed back to the room with the ice sculptures and through the backstage maze to the main front doors faster than I would have thought possible. When you're desperate, you don't get disoriented so easily, I guess.

"Call 911," I shouted at a guy in a goofy red-and-gold bellboy-type uniform who was manning the box office.

"There's been a murder backstage, in the room off the ice rink!"

He did a double take, then picked up the desk phone and started punching in numbers.

Mackenzie and I kept running until we were out on the sidewalk.

"Hurry, Mac!" I yelled. "We've got to get back to the festival. Someone took Vladimira's gun."

"Someone?" Mackenzie shouted, jogging alongside me on Fiftieth Street. "You mean Robbie! He killed her!"

"No!" I said. "We would have heard her scream. And he didn't have time to shish kebab her and get her into that garment bag. But I think he saw who did!"

"He looked terrified," Mackenzie said.

"Bingo. Like he'd just seen a zombie!"

15

Pressure Cooker

On Fifth Avenue the crowds were as thick as curdled buttermilk. A cop stood in the center of the intersection, directing the masses around and through police barricades. I pulled out my phone to call Lieutenant Cooper when I got an incoming call.

"P.C., it's Jesus."

"Yo," I said. "What's up?"

"I've got the name of the moneybags behind L'Aventure. It was mentioned in an article in an online restaurant-business trade rag," he said. "You'll never guess."

"Ronald Crumfeld," I said, taking a stab at it.

"Hey! How'd you know that?"

"I put two and two together and got a millionaire," I said.

"Did you know this, though? Crumfeld's shutting the place down. He's getting rid of Julius LaCroix, and putting all his dough into his new restaurant, Willow at the Edge of the Forest."

"I didn't know that," I said. "But it explains a lot. Thanks, Jesus."

I hung up the phone and told Mackenzie what Jesus had just told me.

"So who took the gun from Vladimira?" she asked. "Who's the killer?"

"Think about it," I said, leading her deeper into the pulsating crowd. "Who would stand to gain most from Billy Rose's death?"

The crowd surged around us as we wormed our way closer to the *Gourmet Zone* set, where Julius would begin performing in just a few minutes. With the spectators jammed shoulder-to-shoulder half a block from the stage, there was no way we were going to be able to get up to the set. Instead, we clawed our way to the building opposite and went up to Lieutenant Cooper's temporary station on the second floor.

Near the big picture window overlooking the *Gourmet Zone* set stood Lieutenant Cooper himself, along with Deborah Hudson, Danny Moran, and several uniformed cops.

"Murdered?" Lieutenant Cooper was saying into his walkie-talkie. "Skewered through the neck with a sword and then hung in a garment bag? . . . Okay, sergeant, I'll send some men over to Radio City pronto. . . . Ten-four."

"We know who did it," I said, running up to Lieutenant Cooper. "We know who's been killing the great chefs of New York. You've got to stop the show! We know who the murdering zombie is!"

"Now, hold on a minute, P.C.," said Lieutenant

Cooper. "Calm down. Tell me why you think we should stop the show—"

"Stop the show?" Deborah interrupted. "It's the *Gourmet Zone*! It's the centerpiece of the whole fest! We're going on live TV in three minutes! Live national TV!"

"You've got to stop it, Lieutenant Cooper!" I pleaded.

"Now hold on a minute, P.C.," said Lieutenant Cooper, raising his hands in a "caution" gesture. In one of them he gripped the squeezy ball. "I can't shut everything down just because you ask me to, even if you do think you know who the killer is."

Mackenzie and I looked out the window across the street to the *Gourmet Zone* stage. Julius stood behind the set's counter. He wore a chef's hat and a starched white apron—his customary uniform when filming his show. Gofers and techies rushed about the staging, making last-second preparations for the filming. Robbie McGrath touched at Julius's face with a powder puff, and whispered instructions to him. Julius nodded, and said something back to Robbie. They looked up to where we were standing.

"I wonder if they can see us through this smoked glass," I said to Mackenzie.

I waved. They didn't wave back.

A large clock at the side of the stage, just out of camera range, counted down the minutes to airtime. Less than a minute to go.

"Okay, P.C., tell me what you know," said Lieutenant Cooper joining us at the window. "I won't promise you I'll stop the show—but I'm willing to listen to what you have to say."

"Robbie McGrath's got a gun," I blurted out.

Lt. Cooper stared out the window. Across the street, Robbie raced back and forth, motioning to techies to clear the set. The clock showed fifteen seconds to airtime.

"It doesn't look to me like he has a gun," said Lieutenant Cooper.

It was true. Robbie was wearing a tight T-shirt and formfitting white trousers. In that outfit, there was really nowhere he could've been hiding a pistol.

"He's hidden it onstage somewhere," I said. "I'm certain of it."

"Why would Robbie McGrath want to hide a gun in the *Gourmet Zone*?" Deborah Hudson asked, approaching us at the window. Danny Moran was right beside her.

"Yeah, kid. How come you think he's packing?" he asked.

"He's planning on killing Julius LaCroix," I said. "Out of kindness. Out of love."

"You're way out of line, now, P.C.," said Lieutenant Cooper. "What you're saying makes no sense. People don't go around killing other people to be nice to them."

"In this case they do," I said.

"Are you saying Robbie's the zombie killer?" the lieutenant asked.

"Not at all," I said.

"Then what—" Deborah Hudson began.

"Just listen, and let me explain," I said. "Julius killed Billy Rose. Why? Because Ronald Crumfeld, the money man behind L'Aventure, is going to shut down that restaurant. Now, Julius had known that for some time, of course—but that was okay, because Crumfeld had promised, or at least implied, to Julius that he would be put in charge of his newest restaurant, Willow at the Edge of the Forest."

"What's that got to do with Billy Rose?" Lieutenant Cooper asked.

"Crumfeld had a change of heart. He must have heard that Julius was losing his touch. The only reason people were still going to L'Aventure anymore was for his famous Crawfish Julius, and that wasn't enough to base a whole new multimillion-dollar gastronomic palace on. Crumfeld stuck his finger up and figured out which way the wind was blowing. Billy Rose was the rising star of New York, the hot new property. So Crumfeld double-crossed Julius and offered Willow at the Edge of the Forest to Billy."

"I had no idea," Deborah Hudson said.

"No one did," I said. "Least of all Julius. But that's what Billy was telling Julius at the Plaza, just before he was poisoned. And to add insult to injury, Billy told Julius he had figured out the secret to Crawfish Julius—oil of St.-John's-wort."

"Don't people take St.-John's-wort to feel less anxious?" said Lieutenant Cooper, squeezing his stress ball. I wondered if the lieutenant shouldn't try some out himself.

"Exactly," I said. "It's an edible herb that's also a powerful antidepressant. You know how they say that one bite of Julius's crawfish pie makes the world seem like a friendlier place? Well, that's not the flavor, that's the St.-John's-wort. Billy told Julius that he was planning on making 'Crawfish à LaCroix as an homage to him at Willow at the Edge of the Forest."

"Homage, my foot!" said Danny Moran. "Sounds to me like the punk was gonna steal the old coot's recipe!"

"That's how Julius took the news too," I said. "Billy had stolen his restaurant *and* his most cherished secret recipe. So Julius snapped. He staggered back—it's all on the festival tape—and put his hand on one of the planters full of oleander. He knew everything there was to know about herbs and plants. He knew oleander was a powerful poison, and . . . and so he decided in that moment to kill Billy. To put oleander into the salad. . . ."

"Crawfish Julius couldn't have meant so much to him that he was willing to kill a man over it," said Lieutenant Cooper. "Look."

We stared across the street. Julius had lined a baking dish with dough—dough that looked exactly like the mask of the zombie killer.

One of the cops turned up the sound on a nearby television. Glancing back and forth between the live Julius on the stage below, and the televised Julius in the box, we heard him say, "And the next ingredient in my famous Crawfish Julius is butter—half a stick . . ."

"Oh my god!" said Mackenzie. "He's giving away his final secret!"

"He's more desperate than I thought!" I said. "Lieutenant Cooper, you've got to stop the show immediately!"

"P.C., I'm sorry, but you're just not convincing me there's danger to anyone," said Lieutenant Cooper. "Okay, so he's finally going to reveal his secret recipe. Is that a crime?"

"No, but the murder of Paul Zachary was!" I said, almost shouting. Julius wasn't the only one who was desperate.

"Why would Julius murder Zachary?" Lieutenant Cooper asked.

"Because if you watch Zachary's face on the video shot by the German tourist, he cringes *before* Billy swallows the forkful of salad. Zachary had seen Julius put the oleander into the salad. And he let Julius know he was going to blackmail him. The scorpion in the canister was Zachary's little calling card—remember, they'd once owned a bar called the Scorpion Room. We know it was Zachary who put the scorpion in the canister because a pet-store clerk described a man fitting Zachary's description buying a scorpion that very day. And the note Julius destroyed must have been a black-mail note, not an inspector's number. Zachary knew he could at last control Julius, get everything he'd ever wanted out of him—his cooking show, his recipes, his restaurant. . . ."

"But we have film of the person who killed Zachary," Lieutenant Cooper objected. "Julius LaCroix walks with a cane. See? He's practically crippled." He pointed to the TV, where Julius was draining some boiled crawfish at the sink, a cane in one hand. "Zachary's murderer didn't even limp."

"Julius's doctor appointment, right before Zachary's murder, was with his podiatrist, not his cardiologist," I said. "Julius suffers from plantar fasciitis—a painful foot condition, but one that is easily treatable with cortisone injections that temporarily relieve the pain. Julius walked out of the doctor's office not needing a cane. He followed Zachary—and Mac and me—to North-Astor's, where he must have told Zachary to meet him. He had no trouble lifting an eighteen-pound ham and slam-ming Zachary over the head with it, and certainly no trouble shoving a funnel down Zachary's throat."

"But why did Julius kill Vladimira, P.C.?" Mackenzie asked.

"First of all, he never liked her," I said. "Second, he was paranoid about her and Zachary. We saw them talking while Julius did his show yesterday, and Julius probably saw them too. Zachary might have told her what he'd seen. And from the way Vladamira was behaving, it's not unlikely Zachary did tell her. But most importantly, in Julius's desperation, he believed that killing Vladimira would confirm that a madman was using Robbie's cookbook as a blueprint for murder. He was hoping to throw us off the scent by providing a false modus operandi—and it almost worked."

No one said anything for a few moments. On the TV, Julius could be heard saying, ". . . and, the secret ingredient, satisfier of a thousand appetites, soother of a thousand moods . . . oil of St.-John's-wort!"

All of us—Lieutenant Cooper, Mackenzie, Deborah, Danny, the other cops, myself—looked through the window at Julius as he tipped a beaker full of golden liquid into a pastry shell filled with bright-red crawfish.

As the audience applauded, I noticed something sinister on the countertop next to the crawfish pie. I looked at the TV, which gave a clearer view of the counter than I had from across the street. Just as I had thought—a platter full of mushrooms.

"Lieutenant Cooper," I said quietly. "You really, really have to stop the show now—because of the mushrooms."

"What are you talking about, P.C.?" he asked.

"There are no mushrooms in Crawfish Julius. And those aren't portabellos or shiitakes, they're called destroying angels. Chef Julius LaCroix is going to kill himself!"

16

A Wrap, and Hold the Mayo

Mackenzie and I bolted from the room, Lieutenant Cooper and several other cops right behind us.

"This is Cooper!" the lieutenant shouted into his walkie-talkie. "Notify officers MacLendon and Izzard—they're manning the stage. I have reason to believe Julius LaCroix is going to poison himself. We've got to stop him."

We hit the lobby at full tilt and were out the doors in an instant. The crowd was impossible—I felt like a salmon swimming upstream through level-five rapids.

Lieutenant Cooper caught up with Mackenzie and me and led charge. The crowd began parting for him—a big, tall guy flashing a badge—in a way that it had steadfastly refused to do for me.

"Remember," I called after Lieutenant Cooper, "Robbie has a gun! Be careful!"

"I never saw any," Lieutenant Cooper yelled.

"Trust me on this one," I said.

"Oh my god!" Mackenzie screamed. "Julius is eating the mushrooms!"

"Oh no!" I shouted. "Destroying angels are the most poisonous of all mushrooms. A single bite has enough toxin to kill him!"

Lieutenant Cooper broke through the front of the crowd and leaped the police barrier holding people back from the stage. Mackenzie and I made like Edwin Moses and were over it too.

A young man holding a clipboard tried to grab Lieutenant Cooper, shouting, "You can't go up there, we're filming!" but the lieutenant brushed him aside.

We were now within ten feet of the stage. Looking up, I saw Julius, an expression of terror mixed with confusion on his face. Seeing the lieutenant coming at him, he grabbed a fistful of mushrooms and stuffed them in his mouth, chewed once, and swallowed the deadly mass in a single gulp.

"Cut! Cut! Go to commercial!" screamed the guy with the clipboard, as complete chaos descended on the stage. Uniformed cops, various techies, even some members of the audience rushed the stage.

Julius clutched his chest, dropped his cane, which clattered onto the floor, and a moment later he collapsed.

"Oh, my God!" someone screamed. "He's having a heart attack!" Lieutenant Cooper ordered two of his men to grab Robbie McGrath, who had rushed to Julius's side. They held him by the arms and frisked him, finding nothing.

Julius, barely conscious now, was reaching out a frail hand to Robbie.

"Let him go," I said to the cops holding Robbie. "It's his father. His father is dying."

Robbie knelt by the dying chef's side.

"I'm sorry it had to end this way, Robbie," Julius wheezed. "I cherished you. You meant more to me than . . . food itself."

He closed his eyes, and his body went limp. Robbie hung his head and wept.

By this time several dozen uniformed officers had arrived on the scene. They cleared the stage, pushed the crowd back, told people to move along, the show's over. Medical personnel arrived and started working on Julius, but to no avail. He was dead.

Lieutenant Cooper took Robbie by the arm and started to lead him away. "We're going to the precinct house," he said. "I'd like you to answer some questions for me."

Robbie nodded. He looked utterly destroyed.

Before they left, I went up to Robbie and said, "I know what was going on, what you meant to do. You should just be glad you weren't able to."

He looked at me. His eyes welled, and he nodded. No more needed to be said, and Lieutenant Cooper took him away.

"What was that about?" Mackenzie asked. "What did you mean, you knew what he meant to do. I thought you said he was going to kill Julius."

"He was," I said. "I think Robbie suspected from the start that Julius was the killer. By the time Vladimira was killed, he was sure of it—he saw Julius do it. But Robbie was smart enough to know that Julius would never get away with it. Things were unraveling before their very eyes. He was going to kill Julius to save him the disgrace of being exposed as a murderer."

"And Julius wanted to save Robbie, too," said Mackenzie. "By killing himself before Robbie had the chance to."

"Right."

"But where's the gun?" Mackenzie asked. "You said Robbie had Vladimira's gun."

I led Mackenzie over to the set's countertop, where there was a platter full of rolled-out sheets of dough, like the one Julius had used to make his crawfish pie— and to cover his face as a mask.

"What?" said Mackenzie. "That's only some old dough."

I lifted up a corner of the dough. Peeking out was the snub-nosed nickel-plated barrel of Vladimira's pistol.

"Oh," said Mackenzie.

"Yes," I said. "A recipe to die for."

Three hours later, Mackenzie and I were sitting around her apartment, waiting for our takeout Chinese food to be delivered. In the past two days I'd heard enough about caviar and braised pheasant and coconut mousse with vanilla-orange compote to last me a lifetime. I wanted plain old pork fried rice and General Tso's chicken. Mackenzie ordered the veggie subgum. The food arrived. All was right with the world.

"How did you figure out that Julius was the killer, P.C.?" Mackenzie asked, skillfully picking up a snow pea with her chopsticks.

"It wasn't easy." I scooped up a forkful of rice—no chopsticks for me. "What I happened to know about zombies helped me crack the case. Wearing dough for a mask is something any of one of our chef suspects could have thought of—if nothing else, because it was so convenient for all of them. But the more cases we take on, and the more I study the criminal mind, the more I've begun to believe that nothing ever happens without some reason behind it, as insane as it may seem at first. Because there was another reason why Julius would choose a mask of dough—why he would choose to look like a zombie when committing a monstrous act."

"Why's that?"

"Well, there's only one place in America where there are conjure men, and voodoo, and a widespread belief in werewolves and zombies and other supernatural monsters."

"Louisiana," Mackenzie said. "Julius was from Louisiana."

"Right," I said, finishing off my plate of spicy chicken. "You can't grow up in Louisiana without hearing about the walking dead. And isn't that what Julius was? He'd come to the end of the line long before this year's festival. Billy was just the last straw—and so Julius snapped."

"It's a sad story," Mackenzie said.

"Murder always is."

"And now we'll never get a top-of-the-line chef to cater our sixteenth birthday," Mackenzie said. "I mean, in the last two days we've met all the top chefs in New York, and the ones who didn't wind up dead aren't exactly chomping at the bit to do us any favors."

"Oh, I don't know. I think Danny Moran kind of liked you."

"Please. What a creep. He and the Ice Princess deserve each other," Mackenzie said, cracking open a fortune cookie. "I know it sounds trivial, given everything that's happened, but still—it's disappointing that we won't have a fancy chef do our party."

"It is," I said, though I thought she was probably feeling a lot more disappointed than I was.

"So what kind of food *are* we going to serve at the birthday bash?" she asked.

"I don't know." Changing the subject, I asked, "What does your fortune say?"

She unfolded the little strip of paper and read aloud: "'Trust your intuition. The universe is guiding your life.'"

"That's nice," I said. "So what's your intuition telling you, Mac?"

She looked at me thoughtfully. "I think we've—or maybe I should say, *I've*—been too worked up about wanting to throw the coolest, greatest blast ever, just so I could impress everyone at school. That's no reason to throw a party just to make other kids jealous. We should serve the kind of food *we* like—fried rice and vegetable subgum, for instance, not snails or whatever it is a fancy chef would make. Let's do that, P.C.—serve good old Chinese food. Everybody loves it, and it makes everyone happy."

"I think you're on to something there, Mac." I cracked open my own fortune cookie.

"What does yours say?"

"'You will eat a fortune cookie,'" I read. I laughed, popping the cookie in my mouth. "Now how did it know that?"

"The universe must be guiding your life too," said Mackenzie.

CHECK

OUT

THE

NEXT

P.C. HAWKE

MYSTERY. . . .

From the terrifying files of P.C. Hawke:
THE PHANTOM OF 86TH STREET • Case #8

Mackenzie and I slowed down as we approached the Eighty-fifth Street exit from the transverse through Central Park. The blindingly bright-red ambulance lights strobed the intersection. There were about half a dozen cop cars on the scene. Not to mention the taxi, white van, and late-model Honda that were strewn about the intersection. Steam poured from the taxi's hood, which was crunched in practically to the windshield. The van had jumped the curb and was on the sidewalk of the uptown side of Fifth, facing downtown. Across the street from the van, the Honda was wrapped around a lamppost.

Inside the open back of one of the ambulances, a medic was taking the pulse of a middle-aged lady with a bandage on her forehead. We could hear her saying, "I didn't see her! She darted out of nowhere! The next thing I knew . . ."

"Come on," I said, tugging on the picnic basket. Mackenzie followed.

We forced our way through the crowd that had

gathered on the corner and saw the body of a woman lying facedown on the curb. From the unnatural position of her arms—palms up, right hand flung across the small of her back—it was obvious she'd been hit at great speed. A paramedic was kneeling over her, but she was dead.

"What happened?" I asked the heavyset guy in a Mets cap who was standing next to me.

"Don't know, buddy," he said. "She got whacked by the taxi, I think."

A man in a blue nylon NYPD jacket pushed through the crowd and hollered at us. "Show's over. Go home, before I run you down to the station for loitering."

A uniformed cop came over and said, "Lieutenant Douglas, we got the Eighty-sixth Street transverse closed off."

"Thank you, sergeant," said the lieutenant. He shook his head. "Nutcases ought to be in Bellevue, not out on the street where they can hurt themselves. Ran screaming straight into traffic and ate a bumper. Guess it's what the voices told her to do."

Most of the crowd had dispersed by now. But Mackenzie and I knew that the lieutenant had a lot better things to do than arrest anybody for loitering. So we stuck around, to see what we could see. After a few minutes, the paramedic guy who'd been examining the dead woman wandered over to a nearby ambulance.

"Here's our chance," I said to Mac. "Drop the basket, and let's take a closer look."

We put the picnic basket in the doorway to an apartment building, then walked casually over to the body. I knelt down to take a better look at her. Since she was facedown, it was hard to tell how old she was. She had long, straight brown hair, and she was wearing a stonewashed denim jacket and blue jeans.

"Take a look at this, Mac," I said. She knelt down next to me. "Cuts on the back of her neck—you can see them through her hair." I really wanted to brush her hair out of the way, to take a better look, but I didn't want to disturb any evidence.

"Her jacket is slashed too," Mac said, pointing to several cuts that ran from just below the collar down between her shoulder blades to about midway down her back.

"Looks like she was mauled by a saber-toothed tiger," I muttered.

"Those are some pretty strange marks to be on someone who was hit by a car."

I nodded. "Exactly what I was thinking."

Just then the paramedic guy returned. "Hey, kids, move along. You don't want to look at her. You'll get nightmares."

"We've seen worse," I assured him. And it was true, we had seen worse—far worse. Mackenzie's mom, the chief coroner, had let us accompany her to her job at the city morgue.

"Sure you have, kid," said the paramedic, draping a long sheet over the body. "Sure you have."

It wasn't worth it to argue with the guy.

We scanned the group of witnesses waiting to be interviewed by the cops. Lieutenant Douglas was talking to a matronly lady with a vicious-looking Pekingese tucked inside her fur-trimmed coat. The rat-dog snarled and snapped at anything that came within four feet of him.

Nearby, a very tall, very thin man wearing a red, black, and green knit hat was yelling into a cell phone. "It wasn't my fault, man!" he said. "Insurance will cover the damages. . . . Yeah, man . . . Okay, okay."

I waited till he hung up, then walked up to him.

"You the driver?" I asked, pointing to the taxi, which was still emitting steam gustily.

"My cab, yes," he said.

"Can you tell me what happened?"

He looked surprised. "You're young to be a policeman, little man."

I smiled and shook my head. "Not a cop. Just an interested civilian."

The man smiled back. "If you say so."

"So what did you see?"

"Not much, man. It happened so fast. I just dropped off a fare. All of a sudden this woman, this crazy woman, she just jumped in front of my car. Crazy expression on her face—huge eyes. Like she'd seen a ghost, you know?"

"Or a phantom," I said.

"Yeah, man, a phantom. She was coming right at my windshield. I slammed on the brakes and closed my eyes. Then I heard a big *whap*, like the sound of a cricket bat smacking a side of beef, you know?"

"Sure, sure," I said, though honestly I was having a hard time imagining it.

"Ooh, it was terrible."

The poor cabbie looked like he was on the verge of tears. I patted him on the shoulder and said, "It wasn't your fault. There was nothing you could have done."

"Thanks, man."

I looked around at the crowd of witnesses, onlookers, and cops and grabbed Mackenzie by the arm. "Mac! We have to stop him!"

"Who?"

"Follow me!" We ran over to where Lieutenant Douglas was motioning to the paramedic guy to take away the body of the woman. A small circle of uniformed cops was standing around the lieutenant. A walkie-talkie crackled loudly. One of the cops was saying, "So then my no-good brother-in-law—"

"Lieutenant!" I shouted, bursting into the circle of cops.

"What do you think you're doing, buddy?" the cop asked as I tried to get the lieutenant's attention.

"I need to talk to—"

"Move along," the cop said, slapping his nightstick against the palm of his hand. "We're busy here." He turned and said to one of the other cops, "So anyway, my wife gave the lazy bum two hundred—"

"But—" I started up, and the cop faced me again.

"Listen, pal—" he said, poking me in the solar plexus with the butt end of his nightstick. At that moment, Lieutenant Douglas stepped between us and said, "Cool your jets, Hansley."

The cop muttered "punk" under his breath and turned back to his buddies.

Lieutenant Douglas turned to me. "Okay, kid. What do you want?"

"Those people over there are trampling a crime scene," I said.

The lieutenant shook his head. "There's no crime scene here. This was an accident."

"It was homicide," I insisted. "I'm sure of it."

DATE DUE